Just the right name...

Now it was time for Sarah's kitten. Sarah watched the little black cat scamper away to bat at the broomstraws, white paws flashing. Then the kitten stopped and sat neatly, staring at the broom, not moving. . . .

"What do you think your name is?" Sarah said to her kitten. "Are you Cat?"

Slowly, slowly, the kitten reached a paw toward the broom—and then darted a scratch at it before the broom could fight back.

"Oh, my little bug." Sarah laughed. "Oh!"

For there it was: Lilybug. A name funny and dear like the kitten, delicate and humorous by turns. And when her kitten was grown, if she became a lovely, serene cat, she could be Lily. . . .

The House Of Thirty Cats

by

Mary Calhoun

AN ARCHWAY PAPERBACK
POCKET BOOKS . NEW YORK

POCKET BOOKS, a Simon & Schuster division of
GULF & WESTERN CORPORATION
1230 Avenue of the Americas, New York, N.Y. 10020

Published by arrangement with Harper & Row, Publishers, Inc.
Library of Congress Catalog Card Number: 65-11454

ISBN: 0-671-42064-X

First Pocket Books printing February, 1970

15 14 13 12 11 10 9 8 7

Printed in the U.S.A.

IL 4+

The House Of Thirty Cats

CHAPTER ONE

At the end of the street was the house. She sat on the curb across from it, not looking at it.

For a moment she watched the black cat slipping through the tall grass far out in the field beyond the house. His tail slunk behind him, not up like a happy cat's tail. There was something ugly about the way he moved that didn't fit with her feeling about the house. It made her even more uneasy. No, she wouldn't look at the house yet. She dipped her head to let her hair slide forward in a curtain around her face, a shimmer-curtain with only herself inside.

What should she say? I'm Sarah Rutledge—I've come—I am Sarah. "Sarah," she said aloud, listening to the sound of it. A dull name, Sarah. Was she like her name? "Sar-ah." It moved slowly. "Ss-ar—" A shushing, silvery sound, perhaps? Silver-gray? Ah, nice. "I am slow and silver-gray," she said, trying it. Dove-gray? Pussywillow-gray, plushy soft with a fresh sheen, kitten-gray?

But mostly I am plain gray.

Sarah sighed, and her hair swayed. This wasn't getting anything decided about the house. It was always like this. While she was thinking (daze-dreaming, Papa called it), the other girls were hurrying on to do something else or getting their lessons done. And if she did try to tell the girls some of her ideas, they thought she was silly, babyish, stupid. Like the time she'd said she believed in fairies. They just laughed. But she'd meant only that there *might* be fairies in the world, little butterflylike creatures. Nobody had ever proven there *weren't* fairies.

Once she'd had a friend. Kerry. They'd imagined together. Kerry was quicker to think of things, but it was Sarah who worked out the details. They'd made flower dolls together and once a rock-garden town, tiny, with pebbles to outline. There was even a little Japanese bridge. . . . Kerry had moved to another town more than a year ago. Since then there'd been no one. That was why Mother finally had said she could have a cat.

Carefully Sarah did not look at the house. She watched the drops of sunlight shimmering on her curtain of hair. So nice here inside. No one to laugh at what she said. Of course there were people she loved: Mother, who worked afternoons as a doctor's receptionist; Papa, who made up beautiful pages of type in his printing shop; Bets-C, her big sister, who was always laughing with girls or talking on the phone with boys; and her younger brother, Harry, who rushed along in a crowd of boys, who ground his teeth in his sleep at night. There were people whom she liked, too: her teacher, the butcher, Lucy at school, who was a very kindhearted girl. . . . But really there was no one just her own. That was why the cat. She'd asked and asked Mother, until Mother said, yes, if Sarah would feed it and vacuum up the cat hairs, she might have a cat.

A cat . . . she cradled the furry idea of it in her mind. But first it must be a kitten. Then it would grow up just hers, she and the cat would be friends from the cat's beginning.

And the cat must come from the house. That would make the cat so perfectly right, to come from the house. Yet—oh, how to decide?—she might spoil everything if she went to the house.

Sarah took a big breath and found she'd been breathless, the pressure of having to decide was building up so. She'd planned not to look at the house at all until she'd decided, but suddenly she couldn't wait one more minute. She lifted her head, and her hair slid back behind her hair band. Now!

And there it was, the House of Thirty Cats.

A little old white house, it was, with apple trees. And yellow daffodils growing helter-skelter in the grass at the corners of the yard. And cats. Cats, cats, cats. Plus one small old lady. For there lived Miss Tabitha Henshaw and her cats. She had twenty or thirty cats, people said. Sarah had named it to herself the House of Thirty Cats, liking the way the words wove as a cat weaves its tail. The House of Thirty Cats, the one wondersome place that Sarah knew of in this ordinary town.

The house even had the look of a cat to Sarah. It was a two-story wooden house, but not very big, the old-fashioned cottage sort. From one side of the house a picket-railed porch curved around the front, wrapping itself around the house to keep it cozy, like a cat's tail curved around its paws. Two narrow pillars outlining the front door were the legs of the cat. But the nicest thing was that the house was cat-eared. The roof rose to something of a point, and set into the roof were two dormer windows with their own little pointed roofs. They were the pricked-up cat ears. Except that the house must have sagged somewhere, for one window-ear cocked slightly to one side, a listening cat ear. Though the white paint was faded and peeling, the house had a happy look to it, an old cat with shabby fur but comfortable with years of purring.

It was a good place for cats, lots of room around the house. Beyond it stretched open fields and woods. On the side toward town was a big yard, then a row of high lilac bushes that separated it from the next house. In the side yard were old apple trees and one great mulberry tree, with a weathered gray stable at the back.

And there were the cats. You didn't see them all at first. The place was like the puzzle pictures where you hunt the hidden faces. Sarah made a game of picking out the cats. There were two cats chasing across the grass and a cat sunning on the front steps. Those were easy. And there was a cat inside the front window, lying out long on a couch back. Quick, was that a cat face at a dormer window? Too late to know. There, up in an apple tree, was a cat creeping along a gnarled branch. Was it sniffing the April buds? Stalking a bird? Scrambling up the mulberry trunk, a cat. Crouching under the new leaves of the lilac hedge, a cat. And there through the hedge slipped another cat to the neat flower beds of the house next door. Delicately that cat sniffed at a late daffodil dipping in the breeze, and then just as delicately the cat took a nibble of the daffodil.

Cats, cats, sunning and snoozing, climbing and exploring. But no kittens. No cat really small enough to be called a kitten. There had to be a kitten. In all those thirty cats, surely there was a kitten for her. She'd waited so long, wanted one so long. . . . Oh, now, how to decide? Should she ask for her kitten here? But if she did, maybe she'd find out that the place wasn't special at all. She might lose the wonderful feeling of the House of Thirty Cats.

The world Sarah knew was hamburgers-and-onions and arithmetic lessons and brushing-your-teeth. Just an ordinary world with everything right out in the open where you knew pretty well what would happen next. Church on Sunday, wash on Monday, some things nice, some dull, but all very everyday.

Not so at this house of cats. Surely not . . . When she was little, Sarah was always hoping to find a magic place. Now she knew she'd never come upon a stone tower rising unexpectedly in the woods or a hut where lived a strange little man. But this house of cats WAS, it existed. And any place where so many cats lived just had to be wondersome.

Almost an enchanted place, it seemed to Sarah, a place where anything might be possible. It was a mystery, a door open a crack into—what? It was a mystery, but not exactly a mystery you wanted to settle. The way it was with a haunted house. You could say, "Look, there's that old haunted house," and shiver deliciously. But if you actually explored the haunted house someday and found it was only a dirty, empty old house, then you'd have nothing left. Nothing to imagine about. So, as with a haunted house, the House of Thirty Cats was a mystery, a place of strangeness. Ever since she was little she'd loved the feeling the place gave her. But now if she went into the house, found out about it, she might lose the feeling of some lovely unknown.

For no one else in town thought the place was wonderful. They said Miss Tabitha Henshaw must be crazy. Look at the way she lived alone with all those cats and the way she dug dandelion greens along the edges of people's sidewalks. They said that with all those cats the house must be nasty inside, wallpaper clawed from the walls, cat mess all over the floors, stinking of cats. No one seemed to know much about the inside of the house, for Miss Tabitha Henshaw lived alone with her cats. She never asked anyone in.

She must have lived there all her life, for everyone knew of her. Once in a while you'd see the little old lady slipping along the streets in her long black cloak or digging her greens, and you'd say, "There's Miss Tabitha Henshaw." It was always the full name, never just "Miss Henshaw." Though once at the meat market Sarah had heard the butcher call her "Miss Tabitha."

The other children were rather afraid of her.

Sometimes they'd go to her house for a cat. But it was as if the old lady might be scary or mean or a witch. They'd stand on the porch and say rapidly, "Please-may-I-have-a-cat?" and then maybe she'd put a cat in a child's hands, and they'd all run away fast.

Ah! That's what she'd do. She'd ask for the kitten on the porch, not go into the house at all. Just exactly that. Then she wouldn't find out a thing about the house. It would still be a mystery. She could keep her feeling about it.

Sarah hurried across the street before she could change her mind. And the cats disappeared as if by magic. When she reached the yard, the only cat in sight was the fat white one snoozing on the front steps like a good-natured Keeper of the Gate. He gave Sarah a friendly "meow." But suddenly he stiffened, looking intently beyond her, the white hair rising along his backbone.

It was the black cat. There, crouching in the shadow of a bush, was the black cat Sarah had seen in the field grass. His eyes were yellow slits in the black fur, and his sides were sunken. He moved, a creeping movement, the grace of a cat changed to a slinking.

Stepping carefully, the white cat sniffed up to the black one and— There was a quavering moan— it happened so fast—a paw— Sarah wasn't sure which cat attacked. Howling, snarling, black and

white tangled. Sarah cried out, then screamed. For she saw the black cat's sneakiness turn to savagery. His sides might be gaunt, but his shoulders were heavy, his claws extended to gouge. He was trying to kill this comfortable old white cat.

Sarah rushed to the door and pounded on it. Oh, hurry, hurry, she prayed. If this was what the House of Thirty Cats meant—death in a sunny morning—Hurry!

No one came. A cat shrieked in pain. The white one? There was red on the white fur. The black cat seemed all gashing teeth. If the white cat died it would be her fault.

Sarah ran to the cats, kicking into the struggle,

trying to kick the black cat away, sobbing "Stop it! Stop it!"

And then there was a little woman beside her, beating at the cats with a rolled umbrella. The black cat leaped free and hurtled toward the field. The white one lay on the grass for a moment, sides heaving, then gathered himself up and limped to the porch. The old lady followed him.

"Now, Peter," she soothed, picking him up and looking him over. "Just a scratched leg. You'll be all right, Peter. Shame on you, fighting with a poor homeless cat." She gave him a spank.

Sarah was confused. Now she wasn't sure what she'd seen at first. Had Peter really attacked an intruder, who'd only defended himself? But the black cat—

"No!" she protested. "He was wild—he was going to kill—"

The old lady turned on her, and her soothing voice changed suddenly to a scratch. "What do you mean, kicking those cats? *You'd* more likely kill poor Peter, kicking like that— Oh, I'm sorry, you're bleeding." Her voice softened again. "Your ankle is scratched."

Sarah stood without words. This little Miss Tabitha Henshaw *was* strange, just as people said, so angry and scratchy one minute, so soft the next. She had a spatter of white curls and a wrinkled face, but it was her eyes that caught Sarah's attention. They were brown, and they were soft and big like a young woman's, not the hard nuts that old people's brown eyes usually are.

"Let me wash the scratch," the old lady was saying.

Oh, dear, everything had gone wrong. Sarah tried to get back to what she'd planned to say.

"I'm Sarah—no—please-may-I-have-a-cat? I mean a kitten."

A little smile tipped the old lady's lips. "So you are Sarah-No. Will you be Sarah-Yes? Will you come in?"

"No!" Sarah stepped back. That was just what she didn't want to do.

"Afraid"—the lips sank into wrinkles—"like all the rest."

The word snagged at Sarah. Afraid? She'd seen the hurt in the old lady's face, and she was sorry for that, but there was more. Afraid? She wasn't afraid of Miss Tabitha Henshaw or the house. But she was afraid of something. She was afraid of finding out that the house wasn't wonderful. Yet, on the other hand, it *could* be a wonderful place. And then if she didn't go in, she'd miss it.

Miss Tabitha Henshaw was back inside the house, closing the door.

"Wait!" Sarah cried. "Yes!"

"Then come." And without another word from Miss Tabitha, Sarah was inside the house.

She was inside the House of Thirty Cats, and all she could see was a narrow dark hallway with closed doors to rooms on each side. Her muscles tightened as if she were holding her breath. Was she about to lose it all, the possibilities, the lovely strangeness?

The woman led the way back along the hallway to a door that opened into a shadowed kitchen. In the midst of the shadows sat a large yellow cat staring from yellow eyes. Behind him was a tall cookstove, black iron, with a black pot of something bubbling on it—like a witch's caldron? And then Sarah forgot to wonder about the house and her feeling and Miss Tabitha. For there behind the stove, taking the warmth of the wood fire, was a box of kittens.

"Ah!" Sarah sank to her knees beside the boxful of cats. Here, too, was the blackness of cat fur, but not the blackness of the cat under the bush. Here was purring and contentment. A slender black mother cat lay in the box, her side turned up for her nursing kittens. Lined along her side were three black kittens, all working their tiny paws at their mother's fur to draw out the milk. One was all black, one had black fur that promised to be long, with just the hint of a white ruff under its chin, and one had white spots. A fourth kitten slept curled between its mother's paws. This one was black too, but with white feet and a white stripe up

its nose that made the kitten look alert even with its eyes closed.

As Sarah leaned over the box the mother cat lifted her head anxiously. Sarah smoothed her head, and the cat's interrupted purr swelled again. Satisfied that no harm threatened, she twisted more to her back that the kittens might get at the nipples easily. At her movement the kitten between her paws woke, and its head came up, wobbling. The round eyes were blue and unseeing, as if they'd been open only a day or so; yet the kitten seemed aware of Sarah, looking for her, small head moving.

Oh, the darling! Sarah reached one finger to touch the white stripe on the kitten's nose, and the kitten bobbed back, startled. And tipped over backward in a soft heap between the mother's paws. Immediately, though, the kitten picked itself up, shaking its head because that wasn't what it had meant to do at all.

Sarah giggled, the sound bubbling in the silence of the kitchen.

"A laugh like a golden curl."

Sarah had forgotten the old lady. She looked around to see her standing in front of the stove, stirring at the black pot.

"Such a nice cat family!" Sarah said.

The woman continued to look into the pot. "So long since a child laughed in this house."

It was as if they weren't talking to each other at all. Sarah tried again.

"Please? Miss Tabitha Henshaw? These kittens are too young to leave home. Are there other kittens?"

At last the soft brown eyes looked at her, remembering that here was Sarah. "Yes, Sarah- Yes, there are bigger kittens," Miss Tabitha said, smiling. "But first let's see to your leg."

She wet a washcloth at the sink and washed the dried blood along the scratch, though Sarah wished she wouldn't bother. Close this way, the old lady had a strange, dry smell, but it was not unpleasant. She hadn't wanted to know this old Miss Tabitha Henshaw, yet here she was, with the cat lady washing her leg. You can't just say nothing for a long time while someone doctors your ankle.

"What are the kittens' names?"

"I haven't named them yet. The naming of cats is a very important matter."

"Oh, yes," Sarah agreed. "A cat's name should be like him. It should fit him just so."

Miss Tabitha glanced up, eyes bright. "Exactly. Fit him like his fur. You have to watch a cat awhile to know his name. There even might be one right name when he's a kitten and another when he's grown. A Bouncer might grow up to be a very definite Charles."

Sarah joined with the idea eagerly. "Or a Cuddles might turn out to be Princess when she's grown."

"It's best, though, not to keep changing a cat's name," Miss Tabitha cautioned. "Better to imagine ahead to what the cat will be. If you keep changing his name, he loses his identity to you. Sam, no; Tiger, no; Felix—Pretty soon he's a hodgepodge."

Sarah caught on to the word. Hodgepodge. She looked thoughtfully at the white-spotted black kitten in the box, and then she said, "Miss Tabitha

Henshaw, truly, I think this little spotted one should be Hodgepodge. His colors are all so mixed up, and he's so cute and roly-poly, as if a funny name would go with him."

The old lady laughed, a dry, crickling, small laugh. "Just so. Hodgepodge." She looked again at Sarah. "You're a one with a feeling for cats."

Then old Miss Tabitha Henshaw and young Sarah Rutledge smiled at each other over the box of cats, and the purring rose around them.

"Would you like to meet more of my cat family?"

Sarah said, "Yes." Too late now for holding back. Whatever the House of Thirty Cats was, she was about to find out about it.

First the old lady explained how the cats lived at her house, and Sarah listened in delight at the lovely arrangements. There were the indoor cats and the outdoor cats. There actually were about thirty cats—Miss Tabitha was never sure of the number, for some strayed in and others strayed off—but most of them lived outdoors, sleeping in the stable. Even Peter, the old-timer, preferred to stay outdoors most of the time. Only three were permanent indoor cats. However, currently ten cats were living in the house because Miss Tabitha always brought new kittens in so that the tomcats wouldn't kill them. A mother cat might give birth to her kittens anywhere around the place, but when Miss Tabitha found them she always settled the new family in the box behind the stove to grow safely. All but the most stubborn mother cats were content then to raise their kittens in that secluded spot. Two half-grown kittens from the previous batch behind the stove were still living in the house, and Miss Tabitha said that Sarah might choose one of these for her own.

Sometimes the outdoor cats came inside, too, for friendliness, she added.

"The cats come and go that way," Miss Tabitha explained, pointing to an open door to some cellar stairs. In the cellar a ground-level window was always left open for the cats. The old lady laughed her dry crickle. "I can't be doorman for thirty cats. Opening the door for every meow—ha! But now you must meet Alexander, the head of the house."

Alexander was the yellow cat Sarah had seen on entering the kitchen. He sat with his back to them, ignoring the intruder. He was a great handsome cat, and Sarah saw now that he wasn't really yellow. His sleek fur was more a golden brown, the color of old brass, with swirled patterns on his sides rather than straight stripes. Stretched out on the floor behind him was his most magnificent tail, heavily furred and marked with rings of rich brown.

Alexander sat with his head up, his whiskers

out, and stared ahead at his thoughts. He didn't look around as Sarah approached.

"Don't stroke his head," his mistress cautioned. "Let your fingers dangle by his nose for him to smell."

Sarah came around in front of this king cat and held out her fingers to him. The cat stretched his neck just a little and touched them with his nose. His head went back, and he looked at Sarah out of blank yellow eyes. She had no idea whether he'd accepted her.

"Come meet the others."

Miss Tabitha Henshaw led Sarah through a tiny back hallway. Narrow steps rose from it to the second floor, a door opened onto the side porch, and another door opened into a back sitting room. The sitting room was cozy, just the right size to fit around one old lady and her cats. There was a little Swedish fireplace across a back corner, faced with colored tiles bearing pictures. A small fire just right for a brisk April morning was alive in the cater-cornered fireplace, and beside the fire was a wooden rocker with a cat drowsing on its cushion.

"Meow," said Miss Tabitha to the cat, and the cat answered, *"Mr-r-rt?"* rousing out of her nap.

"Now this is Amarantha, and she's very good for laps," explained Miss Tabitha. "Amarantha, this is Sarah."

Amarantha was a calico cat, dark head and tail, orange mixed in, and a soft white underside. She must have been a beauty when she was younger, but now she was getting fat, a very motherly-looking cat, Sarah decided. She stretched out her fingers, and Amarantha rubbed the side of her chin against them, purring a welcome.

"Say 'meow' to Amarantha," the old lady told Sarah.

Obediently, though feeling rather silly, Sarah said, "Meow."

"Meow!" the mother cat promptly replied.

How nice! Sarah had never known a cat that would answer you.

"Amarantha and I have been talking to each other for years," Miss Tabitha said happily. "Now here is Horace, who's been with me the longest."

A wide arch opened between the back sitting room and the front parlor. Not that it was a stiff front parlor. The small room was nearly as cozy as the sitting room, with fat doily-covered chairs and pots of plants on stands. Lying along the back of a couch under the front window was the cat Sarah had seen from across the street. He was an old grandfather of a cat, gray-striped and fat.

"Horace, here's Sarah."

Horace's tail twitched once, but he didn't waken.

"Horace sleeps most of the time, for he's very old. He's retired," the old lady added delicately.

"Otherwise he'd never allow Alexander to be ruler tomcat of the house. And here is a kitten for you. Her name is Tansy."

Sarah looked quickly. The cat was sitting on a chair back staring out a side window, her tail weaving idly. Tansy was half grown, much larger than the kittens in the box. Her fur was a beautiful black mottled with gold, and she had wide-set black ears. Just then a romping of paws sounded in the hallway.

"Oh, such a noisy Skittles!" The old lady opened a door into the hall. "This is Tansy's brother. They're Amarantha's kittens."

A gray-striped kitten bounced sideways through the door and ran under the couch. Tansy dropped to the floor and stepped daintily, tail weaving, to the couch. A gray paw popped out to dab at her feet. Then Skittles came stiff-legging out, leaped at his sister, and the kittens grappled in play.

"You may have Skittles if you prefer a male."

Sarah looked at the two cheerful rooms, the fire, the cats sleeping and playing. She saw playthings for the cats here and there: a rubber ball hanging on a band from a doorknob to bounce, a tangled ball of yarn on the floor. Such a good place. Not at all the mess people said it must be. No stink, no wallpaper clawed in strips.

"A cat makes a house more cozy," Sarah decided.

"Just so," the old lady agreed.

And then as if to say NO! a terrible screaming of cats arose outside.

"Oh, at it again. Those naughty warriors!" Miss Tabitha threw up a window and called, "Napoleon! Wellington! Bad cats! Now you stop that!"

The screeching continued.

"Well, let's go see," Miss Tabitha muttered.

Sarah followed her out to the side porch and stopped short in dismay.

"It's that black cat again!"

Now he was fighting with a big yellow tom, and the yellow cat was a better match for him than old Peter had been. The cats rolled on the grass, clawing, biting, gouging in such fury that it seemed only the winner could live.

"Miss Tabitha! Stop them!"

The old lady ran into the house, black skirts swishing, and returned with a panful of water. She threw it over the cats, crying, "Wellington, stop that!" Immediately the drenched yellow tom broke away and ran off to crouch under a bush and spit angrily.

But the black cat lay still. He looked slimy, with his fur matted and wet. Without rising he wiggled on the grass toward the old lady. His breath wheezed as he appealed to her with a weak meow.

Miss Tabitha knelt to stroke him. "Ah, poor cat, you're hurt."

One black paw was bleeding, bitten clear through, and the cat's breath came in a panting whistle. For the first time Sarah got a good look at the cat's face, blunt and scarred, with dirt-smeared nose and broken whiskers.

The old lady gathered him into her arms, to Sarah's disgust. *She* wouldn't have touched that nasty cat. And now Miss Tabitha was taking him into the house. Sarah followed uneasily. Somehow she had the feeling it wasn't right.

"Please—I don't think you should. He isn't a nice cat."

"Of course he isn't," Miss Tabitha said cheerfully. "He's a wild wanderer. But any stray may come to me for help. Besides, my Wellington hurt him, so I'm obliged to take care of him. From the way he breathes, I think his ribs are broken. Now here's the sickroom for cats."

They had passed through the kitchen, down the cellar stairs, to a little woodroom partitioned off at the back of the cellar. Next to the woodpile was a nest of blankets, the sickbed for ailing cats. Miss Tabitha placed the cat on the blankets, and he lay pitifully with his eyes closed—looking weak and nasty, Sarah thought.

But Miss Tabitha seemed used to mean-faced strays popping in to visit. "My, such an ugly old black thing," she said briskly. "Smudgy-black as tarnish, mean as tarnation. Aha! The very name for him. This cat is Tarnish."

Naming the cat! As if he were to live here now with the cat family. "Oh, Miss Tabitha, you mustn't keep him! He's not like the other cats. Can't you feel the —"

She didn't have words for the feeling of drawing-in that prickled along her arms. The feeling of a dirty spot of blackness in the bottom of this little white house with its apple trees.

The brown eyes sparkled with yellow points. "Little girl, don't tell me about cats. Cats are my business." Then the old lady smiled. "Stop fretting, Sarah. When Tarnish is well, he'll go on his way. He's that kind."

Meantime, she said, the cat could rest quietly in the cellar until his ribs mended. Sometimes the young veterinarian in town would kindly—for free—look at her sick cats, but she thought all this cat needed was food and a dry place to stay until he got well. He'd lick his bitten paw; the best care for it. He might even find a mouse down here. If ever a mouse got into the house, it would be in this little wood cellar.

"And there's nothing like a mouse to cheer a sick cat!" Miss Tabitha concluded.

Sarah couldn't help smiling at the idea of bringing a mouse instead of flowers to a cat in the hospital.

Not that she'd ever do any favors for this Tarnish cat. She just didn't like him. She was glad to wait upstairs in the kitchen while the old lady's small feet tip-tipped up and down the stairs, taking a saucer of milk to Tarnish. The great tawny cat, Alexander, paced the kitchen, switching his tail angrily, stretching his head through the door to the cellar stairs. He didn't want the stranger in the house either. Sarah didn't think she could stand another cat fight this morning, and she was glad when Miss Tabitha came upstairs and shut the door.

As she went to the stove to stir her pot, Alexander sniffed at the door, then sat down with his back to it. He sat with his eyes half closed, but his tail twitched from time to time. The kitchen was quiet, with only the bubbling in the pot and the small sucking sounds of the kittens in the box. Presently Alexander opened his light eyes and regarded Sarah. He rose and padded over to her.

"Now try smoothing him," Miss Tabitha suggested.

Sarah wasn't sure he would allow such a familiarity. He was such a distant, lordly animal, standing there staring at her. Sarah made her hand firm and smoothed it over the strong head, down the rich-furred back. And then—how wonderful!—

Alexander's tail cocked forward and the base of his tail came against her hand, rather like a handshake.

"I think he's accepting me!" She stroked his back again, and again the proud tail came forward to meet her hand.

"Yes, that's his way if he likes someone."

Alexander ended the formalities by jumping into a rocking chair beside the stove and settling himself, paws tucked under his wide chest. His head was still up, but gradually his eyelids sank over the yellow eyes.

"I hope there's enough," Miss Tabitha murmured, peering into her pot. "Not many scraps left from yesterday."

"What is it?"

Stew for the cats, the old lady said. Every day she boiled up a big stew for the cats, using leftovers and bones from the butcher. She couldn't afford to buy canned cat food for so many cats.

Sarah thought to herself that one little old lady wouldn't have many scraps left from her meals, and she wondered if Miss Tabitha Henshaw had enough money to live on.

"Cats, cats"—the old woman laughed over her pot like a cricket cricking—"they keep me busy! One thing, though, I don't feed every meow and smooth on the leg. Out of the question. The cats eat at the same time and only twice a day."

Of course cats shouldn't have to eat all together, like pigs out of a trough, she said. Each house cat had his or her own dish (Sarah saw six bowls lined along a wall on newspapers), and there were pans in the shed for the outdoor cats. Every morning she filled the bowls and pans with stew, and every evening she filled them with milk, made up from powdered dry milk because it was cheaper.

"Monotonous meals, but once a year, on Horace's birthday in May, we have a party for all the cats." Near-hermit Miss Tabitha Henshaw might be, but now that she was getting used to talking to Sarah she rattled along at a happy clip. "But which kitten do you choose?"

Sarah blinked. Yes, she supposed she should decide on a kitten and go home. Oh, dear, leave this lovely house of cats just when she was getting acquainted with it? And which kitten, Tansy or Skittles? She was sitting by the box of kittens, watching them scrabble at each other for nipples. Even as she'd listened to the old lady, she'd been glad to see that the little white-pawed one was eating now, getting her share. Tansy or Skittles? Tansy was such a lovely cat, rather mysterious, too, and Skittles was such a joy of a clown. But they were so big, half grown. She'd wanted a little kitten, one just ready to leave its mother. A squeak in the box made her notice that one of the black kittens was pushing her own white-pawed one away from the nipples. *Her* kitten. Of course. Really Sarah had known it all along. This was the kitten for her, this little black scrap with its blue eyes that had looked for her.

"I *did* want a very little kitten," she said. "Would it be possible—when she's old enough—Might I have this little white-pawed cat?"

"Ladybelle," Miss Tabitha said to the black mother, "she wants one of your kittens. Is that all right?"

Ladybelle continued to purr, eyes closed.

"Of course you may have that one if you don't mind waiting. It will be three or four weeks before she can leave her mother."

"Aha!" she added, as Sarah's face saddened. "I have it. As you're to have one of Ladybelle's kittens, and as you have a feeling for cat names, you may help name the kittens."

She said Sarah might come to see the kittens in a week to start getting ideas of what their names might be, and the following week they'd name the cats.

Then she wouldn't be saying good-by this morning, not to come back to the house at all. And even though she wouldn't be going home with a kitten today, she could watch her own cat grow. Sarah was too happy to know how to show it.

"Thank you, Miss Tabitha Henshaw," she said

softly, looking at the old lady's skirt, not raising her eyes.

"Now, now. 'Miss Tabitha Henshaw'—too big a mouthful for a child. You call me 'Miss Tabitha.' "

Sarah looked up at the old brown eyes that were young. "Thank you," she said again.

As she moved through the dark hallway to the front door she found it was a good place now, not simply blank, for she knew some of the comfortable cat rooms behind the closed doors. She said good-by to Miss Tabitha and walked down the sidewalk.

And what had happened to her feeling about the House of Thirty Cats? Was the strangeness all gone, the possibilities all known now that she'd seen something of life inside the house? Miss Tabitha was so merry with all her cats, yet so sharp and strange by turns. And there was the black spot of Tarnish at the bottom of the house . . . Oh, but all the delicious details of cat life there, the cat personalities, her own kitten! And still so many possibilities. Yes, the house was a wonderful and special place! Ah, she was glad she'd taken the chance of finding out. The feeling wasn't spoiled.

Perhaps the House of Thirty Cats wasn't exactly enchanted, but Sarah was enchanted with it.

CHAPTER TWO

And then, too, maybe she was just a little bit scornful of the other children. Maybe that's why she didn't have a friend. Maybe that's why she didn't tell things, because the others were too dull to understand about fairies and such. The angry thoughts followed after several girls from Sarah's class had passed her on the street without even noticing her to say "hello," they were so busy laughing. It was such a rainy afternoon the streets were almost empty of people, so how could they have failed to notice her?

Wasn't that Miss Tabitha Henshaw ahead there in her long black cloak? Sarah watched as the small old person slipped into an alley between the brick store buildings. Now why was she going

down that dirty wet alley? Sarah stepped alongside the brick wall and peeked around the corner.

Oh, heavens, Miss Tabitha was poking in a garbage can! She had stopped by the garbage cans behind a café and was stirring around in one with a stick. Sarah's mouth curled in disgust yet in sympathy for the old lady as she picked out a greasy bone and put it in a bag she brought from under her cloak. Next a half-eaten hamburger on a bun went into the bag. Ugh, now she had some gravy-smeared meat *in her hand*. She moved on to the next garbage can, but Sarah couldn't watch any longer.

How could she! She *must* be weak in her head, just as people said. And yet as soon as she thought it, Sarah knew that wasn't true. She understood. It was for the cats. Miss Tabitha was hunting for scraps for the stewpot.

How very poor she must be to do such a nasty, humiliating thing. Though maybe she didn't care. Maybe all she cared about was the cats. Still, she shouldn't have to poke in *garbage cans*.

On the way home in the rainy dusk Sarah thought about all the scraps thrown away at her house. But if she took scraps to Miss Tabitha, she might be offended. Sarah wasn't sure how Miss Tabitha would react to anything, really. Of course she'd never tell the old lady she'd seen her in the alley.

Mother was home from work already, frying chicken.

"Oh, good, chicken!" Sarah exclaimed. Chicken bones with shreds of meat on them would be good for the stewpot.

Mother looked at her in surprise. "Well, Sarah! I didn't know you liked chicken so well."

Oh, dear, now she'd have to eat as if she liked chicken. Yet if she cleaned her bones there wouldn't be as much meat left—if she did take the bones to Miss Tabitha. So many problems. Sarah sighed.

And Mother wanted to know why she was sighing if she liked chicken and declared for the hundredth time that she just didn't understand Sarah. Mother didn't understand about daydreaming, either, so long ago Sarah had given up trying to tell her the things she thought about. When Mother wasn't worrying about something, she was more like Bets-C, laughing and busy on projects with her women friends in her club.

All through dinner Sarah tried to decide what to do about the scraps. Miss Tabitha might be angry about "charity" and never let her come back. Deciding was always such a hard thing. Sometimes she tried to imagine what she'd do if various exciting things happened fast. What would she do if the teacher fainted? She'd probably wonder whether to run for the principal or run to the teacher to try to revive her or run to the drinking fountain for a cup of water. And most likely while she was trying to decide, someone else would take care of matters.

Nevertheless when dinner was over, Sarah jumped up. "I'll clear table," she said, taking the plates.

Her brother, Harry, said, "What are you, some kind of crazy? It's my turn."

"I don't mind."

If she was going to save the scraps, she'd have to get them now. She didn't want to go through explaining everything to Mother. Quickly she put the bones in a paper sack, adding bits of baked potato and the potato skins. She hid the sack under her bed. There now, she had the scraps, whatever she decided.

By the next afternoon after school she felt so sorry for Miss Tabitha—and wanted to see the cats again so much—that she took the chance. It was a fresh blue April day after yesterday's rain. Carrying her greasy sack, Sarah watched a robin rise over a tree and felt herself lift with him. "Aha, robin!" she called after him.

She was glad to see that the old lady was in her side yard with some cats. That made it easier, somehow, than having to knock on the door and summon her from the back of the house. Miss Tabitha saw her and nodded brightly, a gray cat smoothing around her skirts. Sarah started across the grass past the apple trees before she remembered that she hadn't planned what to say.

"I brought some scraps for the cats," she said, handing over the sack. She giggled suddenly at herself. Of course. What else was there to say? So there for planning!

And before Sarah had time to worry whether her laugh was out of place, Miss Tabitha said, "How nice. The cats will be glad."

So easy it was. Nothing at all to worry about, then. Sarah looked up at the apple buds, pink

against the blue sky. Soon they'd be all in white blossom, and she'd see that too!

Alexander came racing across the grass, scrambled up a tree trunk, and swung around a branch, as if he, too, were full of the joy of an April afternoon.

"But no birds in the trees," Sarah observed.

"No, no birds, no bird song," Miss Tabitha said sadly. "Birds seldom stop here because of the many cats. However, I can't have everything, bird song *and* cats." She moved toward the backyard. "Come look at my garden and meet some cats."

She introduced the gray-striped cat weaving

about her legs. "This is Felicity. Felicity means happiness. Felicity, this is Sarah."

Sarah didn't know whether to meow or not, but the cat didn't say anything, so she didn't either. Felicity had neat white paws and a white chest. She seemed a tidy, happy cat who lived up to her name. Sarah smoothed her back, and the gray cat throbbed in purrs under her hand.

"And here is Cozy, Felicity's mother. Cozy had her family in the kitten box before Amarantha."

A cat named Cozy. Sarah liked that. She couldn't help picking up the fluffy gray mother cat, who purred in a soft armful.

Behind the house were more cats. Old white Peter was asleep on the back doorstep, and a smallish black cat with polished fur and white feet picked his way across the grass. Miss Tabitha called "meow" to him, and he meowed back politely. She said he was Mr. Tolliver, a gentleman.

And then they reached the garden, a garden that could happen only at Miss Tabitha's house. For it was a cat's garden, a garden planned just for cats. There were clumps of catnip and tall fronds of tansy leaves, both with their strong smell of wild green that sent cats into ecstasies of rolling. There were gooseberry bushes for cats to hide under, and there were new sprouts of asparagus that would grow into feathers of greenery for kittens to bat.

For the cats' stewpot there were plantings of carrots and onions.

There were flowers for the cats, too. Miss Tabitha pointed out the row of fragile white hyacinths along the stable wall.

"Some cats enjoy the smell of flowers," she said. "They seem to relish a sweet fragrance, though they don't like a scent so strong it smothers. Cozy and Mr. Tolliver love to sniff around the hyacinths. Felicity—you see?—is fond of the more delicate smell of lily of the valley and violets."

Felicity, dear little gray cat, was rolling in the violets nestled next to the house, rubbing her chin lovingly against the flowerlets. Sarah didn't think Mother would appreciate a cat rolling in *her* flower beds.

Later on, Miss Tabitha said, there would be petunias and carnations to perfume the air for the cats. And next month all the cats would be playing under the sweet-smelling lilac bushes.

"But what about the daffodils?" Sarah asked, remembering the scatters of yellow in the corners of the front yard. "They don't smell."

Miss Tabitha laughed. "Those are for me. Because I like daffodils."

Sarah ventured to tease. "I thought you made everything just for the cats."

The white curls shook briskly. "Oh, no, I'm not a servant to the cats. The cats and I, we're companions. And I make them behave if they're nuisances. For, you know, a well-bred cat is a happy cat."

Sarah nodded. She hoped she could raise her kitten to be a well-bred cat.

"And now the scraps shall go into the pot," Miss Tabitha said merrily.

They were almost to the back door when a voice cut across the yard.

"Madam, your cats! I'll warn you only once more!"

An erect white-haired man stood in an opening of the lilac hedge. Miss Tabitha turned back toward him.

"Now, Colonel Mace," she said firmly, "we've discussed all that. As soon as your geraniums are out the cats won't want to come. They smell so bitterly—"

"Nonsense! This horde of cats is a wicked nuisance! I have every right to object to their trespassing."

Despite his anger, his voice was snowy-cold. He had a tall, straight back and a strong, hooked nose, and he looked as if you'd have to oil his throat muscles before he could laugh.

Precisely he enumerated the cats' faults. "They howl under my windows. They beg at the back door. They sharpen their claws on my new fruit tree trunks. They dig in my flower beds—"

"Of course," the old lady interrupted with dignity. "Good cats always go off their own grounds to find a toilet."

Colonel Mace continued angrily, "They break down the flowers. They even *eat* the flowers!"

Sarah smiled, remembering the naughty cat she'd seen nibbling the daffodil in the military row of flowers before his house. But her smile faded into dismay as the cold voice went on.

"Had I known the situation, I should not have moved here. No one in his right mind would live next door to a screeching madhouse of cats. However, there must be laws in this town against maintaining a public nuisance. Everyone will know I'm right. Madam, unless you drastically reduce the number of your cats *immediately,* I shall take steps!"

He turned and strode back to his house.

"Ha, ha, ha. Step, step, step," the old lady mocked shrilly in time with his feet. Then she too turned and hurried toward her house, muttering to herself.

Sarah trailed after her uncertainly, slightly shocked at the way Miss Tabitha had acted, and full of worry.

Miss Tabitha glanced at her face and said, "Yes, I know. I'm childish. I shouldn't let that old man rile me so."

She explained that he was a retired Army colonel who had inherited the house and moved here last winter. He'd fussed about the cats since the beginning, she said, but he seemed to mind them more now that spring was here and his flowers were coming up.

"I should think of him that way, though, a flower man," Miss Tabitha said, cheering up a bit. "A man who likes flowers can't be all bad."

With a nod that closed the matter, she motioned Sarah into the back porch while she took off the rubbers she wore in the damp grass.

Sarah went into the kitchen. And stopped in horror. Tarnish had her kitten! Jaws gripping the neck fur, he was dragging the limp kitten toward the open cellar door. The mother cat was nowhere in sight, and the three other kittens were reared up in the box, tiny hairs standing out on their bodies. As Sarah cried out and ran forward, the black cat's eyes sparked yellow at her, and he growled a low warning.

"Now then, we'll—" Miss Tabitha began cheerily as she came into the kitchen.

Immediately Tarnish relaxed his jaws and began licking the kitten's ears, for all the world like a kindly old mother cat.

"Well, Tarnish, aren't you nice—" Miss Tabitha beamed on him.

"Oh!" Sarah gasped at the deceitfulness of the

cat. He'd changed deliberately the minute Miss Tabitha walked in.

"Oh, you wicked cat!" She snatched the kitten away from him. The kitten perked up right away in her arms, seemingly unharmed, to Sarah's relief.

And that—that *Tarnish* buttered up to Miss Tabitha even more, walking over to her with a breathy purr. It was such a strangled-sounding purr that Sarah was sure he hardly remembered how. Probably hasn't purred for years—if ever, she thought angrily. But Miss Tabitha didn't seem to notice.

"Feeling better, eh, Tarnish?" she said. "Here, have a snick of meat. No, sir, not the bone!" She added to Sarah, "Never give chicken bones themselves to a cat. They splinter, might choke him."

She tore skin and meat off a chicken back from Sarah's sack of scraps and gave it to him. Taking the offering in his mouth, the cat ran down the cellar stairs, tail slinking after him.

"I wish he would choke! How can you give meat to that wicked cat?" Sarah burst out.

Miss Tabitha faced her, eyes grown small. "Young lady," she said, "I will not have you call a cat wicked. That poor wild thing has never learned manners, but that's hardly his fault."

"But he's bad!" Sarah insisted, hugging her kitten closer. "He was dragging her toward the cellar—maybe going to eat—"

"Nonsense! Tomcats don't eat kittens that big. Now, not another word!" Her mouth was a straight line among the wrinkles.

Tears watered in Sarah's eyes at the old lady's harshness. It wasn't fair. No wonder Tarnish buttered up to Miss Tabitha; after all, she fed him. Didn't she ever think *any* cat was wicked?

With the trouble Tarnish had caused, now Sarah didn't know how to talk to the old lady, and Miss Tabitha was silent at the stove, tearing meat scraps from the chicken bones to stir into the stewpot. Looking at the kitten, Sarah saw it watching her, blue eyes no longer blind, such bright eyes quick to see her every move. The kitten opened its pink mouth in a silent mew to her. Ah, little puss. Sarah cuddled the soft thing under her chin, and her heart felt sharp with love. And fear, too, fear for the kitten. For how could it be safe as long as Tarnish was free to come into the kitchen? Sarah wished she could close him into the woodroom, but she didn't dare ask Miss Tabitha's permission now.

Then a gray cat came running up the cellar stairs and into the kitchen. It was Felicity, the cat whose name meant "happiness." She must have come in through the open cellar window. Felicity leaned her smooth body against Sarah's legs, then wove a circle around Miss Tabitha's skinny ankles, meowing a hello to these nice people. She walked a few steps toward the kitchen door into the back hall and came back to her mistress to look up at her face.

"So, Felicity, you want to go upstairs?" Miss Tabitha said.

She opened the door to the back hall, and the young cat padded through and disappeared up the stairs.

Now what was all that about? Why should Felicity want to go upstairs? What was up there? Sarah realized that she didn't really know very much about the life in this House of Thirty Cats. Nor very much about Miss Tabitha Henshaw. This old cat lady and her cats were bound up in their life here; they didn't need outsiders. She didn't belong here.

"I'd better go," Sarah said.

Miss Tabitha looked up, and her eyes softened. "Ah, such a sad face. Fiddle, I'm sorry I was cross. Come now, be Sarah-Yes. Come and sit with me."

The kindness in her face was real. Sarah felt relief spread over her like a warm wave. She *did* want to be an insider at this house of cats. And she did like Miss Tabitha most of the time, despite her strangeness. Sarah shut out the thought that the old lady might scratch again and followed her into the back sitting room.

There the peace of the room soothed her. Old Horace was the only cat in sight, snoozing on the front room couch. A slow fire in the tiled fireplace ticked away through the passing afternoon, and lowering sunrays lit the wall beyond the fireplace in a glow of light. Miss Tabitha poked up the coals into flames and settled herself in the rocker.

"Time to make a lap," she said. "Cats need a lap now and then."

Sure enough, Tansy came tail-waving out of nowhere and jumped lightly into the old lady's black-skirted lap. Miss Tabitha took up some knitting. Tansy watched the moving yarn intently. She pounced her paws at this live thing, catching her claws in the yarn again and again. Not bothered at all, Miss Tabitha knitted on. At last Tansy turned herself around into a ball. She purred, paws tucked in, watching the yarn for awhile until her eyes closed and the purring softened into sleep.

"Tansy tangled your yarn."

"It's all right." Miss Tabitha rocked comfortably. "Half the reason I knit is for the cats to play with the yarn."

According to Miss Tabitha, if you were sitting down to make a lap for a cat, then that's what you were doing. You didn't read a crackling, flapping newspaper over the cat or try to write letters and then worry if the cat nibbled at your pen. When Miss Tabitha made a lap she knit or read a book.

Sarah felt at ease again with the old lady. But she hadn't forgotten that Felicity was upstairs. She had seated herself on a stool where she could see the back hallway, and so far Felicity had not come down the stairs. Sarah was growing more and more curious about what might be going on up there. Some things about this house were still unknown. . . . Well, there was one mystery she might dare ask about.

"Miss Tabitha," she began shyly, "all these cats—how did it happen? I mean, why do you have so many cats?"

The old lady knit several stitches, then said abruptly, "I didn't intend to have quite so many."

She eased a length of yarn from under the sleeping cat and then was silent for so long, knitting, that Sarah thought she was offended. Embarrassed, Sarah turned to look at Horace, who was twitching in his sleep. Then the old lady began to tell her story.

For years she'd cared for her invalid sister, the two of them living together in this house. In those days they'd had just a few cats—"seven or eight when there were new kittens." Horace, Amarantha and Peter were the only ones left from those times. Then when her sister had died she'd had more time and she'd latched on to the idea: she'd make a home for cats. It had been her pleasure to make her house a place where stray cats could find shelter. She'd tried to raise them properly, and at first she'd attempted to find good homes for them. But cats know where they're welcome. More and more strays kept coming, more and more mother cats had kittens, until now the number stayed at about thirty cats.

"And there are other reasons for keeping cats," she said, her voice trailing off.

A mystery again. That seemed to be the way with this House of Thirty Cats, Sarah thought.

She'd find out a bit, and then she'd come again to the hint of something more.

And what of Felicity? What would a nice little gray cat be doing alone upstairs? Was it simply that she'd gone up to sleep on a bed? Actually what could an ordinary cat be doing that would be strange? You're just making fairy tales again, Sarah told herself. Yet the feeling persisted, a feeling colored like pink moonlight . . . something strange and lovely was going on up there.

Sarah shifted on her stool. Then she had an idea.

"Miss Tabitha, may I use your bathroom?"

Let the bathroom be upstairs . . .

Miss Tabitha nodded and pointed. "Up the stairs and at the end of the hall."

Sarah was glad that the stairs had carpet tacked down on the treads. She mounted the steps soundlessly, up the narrow well. What would she find? Her eyes peeped about. And then at the top she felt actually crushed down by disappointment. For the short hallway was blank with closed doors.

There were two doors on one side, one on the other. Only the bathroom door at the end was open. Sarah went down the hall to the bathroom, thinking she'd find Felicity there. There would be some silly explanation. The gray cat would be playing with water dripping into the washbowl. Or foolishly sitting in the bathtub. Or staring at her reflection in the water in the toilet bowl. Sarah had heard of a cat that liked to do that.

But there was no cat in the bathroom. Sarah looked behind the door, got down on her knees to squint under the old-fashioned tub standing on claw legs. No cat.

Then where? In a shadowed corner of the hallway? No, no cat to be seen, nothing at all in the hall except a chest under the window at the front. No place for a cat to hide. She was positive Felicity hadn't slipped down the stairs. Yet she must have.

No point in opening doors—though she didn't dare snoop that much, anyway—for Felicity couldn't have opened a door. Could she?

And then Sarah saw it. On the side with one door the door was different. At the bottom was a small cutout panel on hinges. It would swing back and forth . . . it was cat-sized . . . it was a cat door.

This must be where Felicity had gone, through this panel. It was a room with a cat door, probably for any cat to go in and out as it pleased. For what purpose? What was going on in there? Suddenly Sarah remembered the cat face she'd seen at the dormer window on the day she'd picked out cats in the puzzle picture. That cat must have been in this room. But why?

Sarah put her ear to the door and heard not a

sound. Purring? Was there a purring sound? Very gently she tried the doorknob, only to discover that the door was locked. She got down on her knees and put her hand on the panel to push it open, to peek through.

And then she was ashamed of herself. What right had she to snoop in this nice old lady's house? She wanted so much to know. But it wasn't her right to know this way—not yet.

Feeling like a sneak, Sarah tiptoed to the bathroom and flushed the toilet. As she went down the stairs she wished she dared ask Miss Tabitha about the cat door. But something kept her from it. She stood at the door of the sitting room.

"I'd better go home now."

Miss Tabitha nodded, awake over the sleeping cat. "All right. Come again."

"Yes, I'll bring more scraps."

Then Sarah Rutledge went out the side door, taking the thought of the locked room with her. A room locked in a house that had no visitors.

CHAPTER THREE

There was a beast outside. She was in a drawing room with a grand piano and carpets and tall French windows, and there was a beast outside the windows threatening her. In terror she ran up the stairs, but the stairs grew narrower until she was caught, suffocating in a small place. Then a woman in a white uniform—a nurse?—came along and helped her up out of the small place. And she came into great light. She shielded her eyes from the light, her hand brushed her face—the touch woke her.

Sarah opened her eyes. She was in bed; moonlight lay on her face. Beyond her window the round moon blazed in a clear sky, lighting the air with whiteness, whitening her bed. She'd been sleeping in full moonlight.

I feel moonburnt, she thought. Moonburnt . . . burned by the moon. Everyone knows what sunburn is, a redness. But what would moonburn be? Would it whiten the face? Perhaps it would burn in something that didn't show, a strangeness. "Sleeping in moonlight makes people go mad," she remembered reading in some story. But she didn't believe that. It was the beast-thing in her dream that had frightened her, not the moonlight. The idea of sleeping in moonlight pleased her. It made her feel rather like a princess. Turning over, she sank back toward sleep.

A sound came. Had it been in her dream of the beast? The sound was outside her window, a wavering, rising sound, a howl. Then spits and yowls. Cats.

Sarah slid out of bed and went to the window. The yard below was distinct with night light and sharp black shadows cast by the moon, the moonlight so glittering it seemed it would click if she touched it. A cat stood on the lawn in the light. Another cat ran past it. Black shape detached from black shadow to follow the second cat. That tail slinking out behind—it was Tarnish!

Now the three cats crouched near one another and the yowling faded to a low muttering. As if those three were talking among themselves. One of the cats Sarah recognized as a stable cat from Miss Tabitha's place. Then as suddenly as they'd stopped, the cats ran off together down the street.

Sarah went back to bed, wondering and disturbed. That awful Tarnish must be over his sickness to be yowling around in the night. But why had the cats come here? Her house was six blocks from Miss Tabitha's. The possibility that Tarnish knew where she lived made Sarah pull the sheet over her head.

That was Sunday night. The next afternoon after school Sarah went to the library. Opening books along the shelves, she found a book that would be satisfying to read just now, a homey family story with nothing scary in it. Yet a part of her wanted something else. She read titles along the lines of books, not sure what she was looking for and not finding it. At last she went to the side-by-side desks of the two librarians.

The assistant librarian's nameplate on her desk read MISS THELMA JONES. Sarah felt sorry for the woman to have such a name. "Thelma" was a grayer name even than her own, and "Jones" was colorless. The woman was like her name, mousy and quiet, usually fading back somewhere among the shelves, putting away books.

MRS. ANNE RITCHARD said the nameplate of the head librarian. Mrs. Ritchard was brisk and cool, and she always knew where to find the book you wanted.

". . . something about the moon," Sarah mumbled to Mrs. Ritchard. The librarian turned to the shelves, and Sarah trailed along behind her. "Sleeping in moonlight," she said under her breath. But she couldn't say it out loud to Mrs. Ritchard. The librarian might look at her and wonder and think she was strange.

So Mrs. Ritchard brought out several scientific books about the moon, and of course they weren't what Sarah wanted. She shook her head until Mrs. Ritchard spoke impatiently.

"If you can't tell me what it is you want about the moon, I can't help you. Surely you can find what you need in all these books."

Sarah edged to the check-out counter with her family story. "Well, thank you, anyway. I'll just take this one."

That night she started reading the book, and the part of her that wanted comforting was warmed by the story. The next day after school she set out to do another cozy thing. Sarah was going to learn to knit. Saturday when she'd taken some scraps to Miss Tabitha, the old lady had offered to teach her knitting.

Sarah liked the idea of learning to knit, and the knitting lessons made an excuse to keep going to the House of Thirty Cats. The lessons also made an acceptable reason to Mother for going to Miss Tabitha's. When she'd asked about the knitting, Mother had thought for a while, because she too had heard that Miss Tabitha Henshaw was "queer." But Sarah had told her how clean the house was and how pleasant the old lady and her cats were. Papa, who'd been listening, had said it would please him as he worked to think of Sarah spending her after-school time with cats and an old lady. (Sometimes Sarah told Papa her dreamings, and he always understood, though he was so quiet and sunk in his books and pages of type that it wasn't always easy to talk to Papa.) Anyway, Mother had agreed it would be nice for Sarah to learn to knit. Mother and Papa didn't come home from their work until 5:30, but the children were to come right home from school unless they had a specific place to go. Bets-C often went to the YWCA to swim and Harry to his ball practice, and now Sarah had permission to go to Miss Tabitha's.

Sarah was to knit a pad for her kitten. That's what Miss Tabitha generally knit, large woolly squares for each of her cats to sleep on. She said a cat liked to have a place that was his very own for catnapping. Horace's pad was on the back of the couch, and Alexander's was in the rocker by the kitchen stove because he liked to keep track of Miss Tabitha as she worked. The outdoor cats especially needed the pads to define their own little spots in the stable, and each seemed to know by the smell of the cat hair on the pads which one was his. Of course not all the cats cared about the pads or slept in the same spot always. Cozy might curl up next to old Peter in some sunny corner, or Felicity nap with a loving paw across Oriole's neck. Oriole was a small white female with patches of yellow on her body. She was a silent little creature, slipping quietly among the flowers. It was she who had nibbled Colonel Mace's daffodil.

Saturday, Sarah had met several more of the outdoor cats. There was Bouncer, a friendly orange cat who was to be seen bounding around the yard in high spirits. There was Brumple of the stubby ears, who sat all in a brump because he was mostly gloomy. There were the top-ranking warriors of the yard, Napoleon and Wellington. Napoleon had lived there first and been boss of the outdoor cats. He was a gray cat with strong black stripes, and he stalked about on his striped legs as if he owned the place. Then yellow-striped Wellington had strayed in one day. He invaded Napoleon's territory, and he won the first battle. But the next day Napoleon won. Ever since, they'd been battling for the supremacy of the yard. They'd go for days, ignoring each other and tending to their affairs, then they'd cross paths and the quarrel would be on again. Miss Tabitha said she thought they rather enjoyed their squabbles. Kept them in trim, and neither was permanently damaged.

Thinking of all the cats, on the way to their house, Sarah felt full of silver bubbles. She sang her version of the song about the days of Christmas. "On the first day of knitting, Miss Tabitha gave to me-e-e, One knitting needle and a cat for to sit on my knee!"

Which was foolishness, of course, for you had to have two needles. And she'd have enough trouble learning to knit without a cat pulling at her yarn.

Sarah went to the back door because she liked to go through the garden alive with cats. Colonel Mace was in his yard and gave her a chilly look, but Miss Tabitha admitted her with good cheer. Sarah went straight to the box of kittens. Fearing Tarnish, she was always glad to see again that her kitten was safe. Ladybelle, who'd been curled in the kitchen rocker, dropped to the floor and leaned anxiously against Sarah, then satisfied that the intruder by the box was a friend, returned to the chair. Alexander, sitting in the middle of the braided rug, switched his tail to show he noticed that Ladybelle was on his pad, but he didn't object.

All the kittens were awake and sitting up in an angled row, little flower faces turned up to look at Sarah. Like a flower arrangement of kittens, she thought. She moved her finger back and forth, and their heads followed the motion, alert but still wobbly. Sarah's kitten lifted one white paw and, just as if she were a grown lady cat, chewed at her toes to clean them. Sarah couldn't resist picking her up to love her.

"I can hardly wait to name them," she said. "Have they gone out of the box yet?"

"No, but they've been thinking about it." Miss Tabitha was doing something with flower seeds at the kitchen counter.

Two of the kittens tumbled into play, while the all-black one curled up unto himself at one end of the box. Sarah put her little white-footed bug back into the box, and it sprang into the wrestling match. Sarah was pleased to see that her kitten was the liveliest of the litter, full of spit and vigor. Finally a kitten squeaked in protest, and the tumble broke apart. First Sarah's kitten, then the other two, advanced to the hole cut in the side of the box.

"I think they're going to come out!" Sarah exclaimed.

Head weaving, she was still so young, Sarah's kitten considered the Outside. One white paw reached cautiously out to the floor. . . . Sarah held her breath. Would her own kitten be the first? Ah, the linoleum was cold and slick; the paw drew back.

Then the spotted kitten came up beside her. Sarah's kitten stood up. She wasn't going to let the other get ahead of her. Slowly, putting down her paws inchingly as if they touched water, she stepped through the opening into the Wide World.

And immediately she skidded into a heap on the smooth floor. Sarah giggled, but she didn't touch her. This was the kitten's adventure. The kitten picked herself up and proceeded out around the cookstove, legs not very used to walking, head looking here and there. She sniffed at the stove leg and started back when her nose touched the cold iron. Ladybelle saw her and sat up with a *pr-rting* sound. But the Explorer, young Marco Polo Cat, continued on her journey. Her paws touched the edge of the rag rug, and she stopped to sniff this new thing. Then in the middle of the rug she saw her goal. Straight across the rug she hurried to the great golden cat, sitting tall as a statue. She touched her nose to the tower of his front leg.

Alexander had watched her approach with slanted-back ears, and now he lowered his head to growl a warning. *"Pr-r-rt!"* cried Ladybelle, jumping down from the rocker. Brave with ignorance, the kitten patted a "come play" paw at Alexander's foot. He got up and stalked away to the sitting room, tail jerking in indignation.

"Ah, my proud Alexander," said the old lady

with a laugh. "But soon you'll be teaching the kittens tricks." She told Sarah, "He always acts as if each new box of kittens were a personal insult, but when the kittens are older, he'll take spells of racing around the kitchen with them, and he'll teach them how to handle themselves when they tangle with a big cat."

Ladybelle herded her young adventurer back to the box. Worn out from exploring, the kitten looked for a soft place to curl up. All the kittens crawled over and over one another until they settled to sleep, twined in a heap.

"Hmmm," Sarah sighed in satisfaction.

Miss Tabitha was ready for the knitting lesson now and led the way to the sitting room. "Meow!" Amarantha made room in the rocker for her mistress. "Meow. Are you a good old Amarantha?" Miss Tabitha took the calico cat into her lap. From a sewing stand by the chair she picked out a knitting needle and mulberry-red yarn.

"First you must learn to cast on stitches," she began.

Soon Sarah was happily involved in the awkward mysteries of making a loom with her fingers to weave stitches of yarn onto the needle. Almost every finger had something to do, this forefinger looping over the yarn, that little finger holding it in a crook. She'd never known her fingers could be so *many,* so stiff, so in the way. However, Miss Tabitha proved a patient teacher, and after several unravelings and startings over, Sarah achieved a row of rather odd-sized stitches on the needle. Now it was time to take up the second needle and begin knitting.

"The needle slants in, so," coached the old lady, guiding Sarah's fingers. Being close, her aged smell came to Sarah, reminding her of dried flowers. Sarah's nose crinkled, but she didn't mind the smell. "And around—no, no, you're losing the stitch—this way." The stitch was saved. "There, you've knit your first stitch! Now again. That's right, loop, around—fiddle! Who's that at the door?"

A knocking was sounding at the front door.

Over Miss Tabitha's wrinkled face came the sly look of a little child, and "Humph!" she said. "We just won't answer it."

She went right on helping Sarah's fingers with the next stich. Sarah was startled. One *always* went to the door when someone knocked; one *always* answered the telephone. But Miss Tabitha Henshaw didn't live by other people's rules. She kept Sarah's fingers going along as the knocking hammered louder on the front door.

For that matter, who could it be at the door? No one ever came to this house. Perhaps it was a child wanting a cat. Whoever it was, he was persistent. Footsteps came along the curling-tail porch around to the back hall door. Two men looked in the sitting room window.

"Pshaw! They've seen us." Miss Tabitha unsettled Amarantha and went to the side door.

Sarah put down her knitting. She could hear Miss Tabitha in the hall, and she could see the men through the porch window. That tall white-haired man was Colonel Mace, but the young man? When he spoke, Sarah recognized him. He was Sam Bailey, the veterinarian who had the animal hospital out on the other side of town. She remembered something else: he was also the town dogcatcher and poundmaster.

"May we come in?" he was asking.

Miss Tabitha must not have moved out of the doorway. Her voice came stubbornly, "I don't know. What for?"

"See here, madam!" Colonel Mace began with authority.

But the young man said, "Well, Miss Tabitha, ma'am, I could tell you better sitting down."

"Weak legs, Sam?" However, her voice wasn't as sharp, and she was letting the men in.

They went through to the front parlor because there weren't enough chairs in the sitting room. Sarah stayed on her stool and gathered Amarantha onto her lap to look down at and hold onto when she saw the men eyeing her. Sam Bailey seemed nice enough, with his round freckled face and sandy eyebrows, but she was afraid of Colonel Mace.

The old gentleman had started to sit down in the chair by the window, but Alexander was sitting on its back looking out the window, so the colonel motioned the veterinarian to the chair and sat on the couch. He brushed his pants legs as if he thought he already had cat hairs on them.

Miss Tabitha perched on the edge of a straight chair. "Now what is it?"

"It's about the cats, ma'am." Sam Bailey was brisk but friendly. "People have complained to the town council—"

"The cats must go," Colonel Mace said flatly.

Sarah held tight to Amarantha, her head dipping lower over the cat, afraid to hear what was coming. Miss Tabitha's face set in its wrinkles, but she didn't interrupt the colonel.

He was saying, "I warned you I wouldn't stand for this public nuisance next door to me. Now others in town are complaining of your cats. Those cats are running wild!"

"I know it's natural with spring coming on." The young man was apologetic. He seemed to like Miss Tabitha and be sorry for her.

Not the old colonel. "The nights are hideous!" he declared. "People's backyards are full of screeching cats, garbage cans knocked over, flower beds torn up. Unspeakable!"

Miss Tabitha's voice was calm. "Are my cats unspeakable, Sam?"

The veterinarian was caught smoothing Alexander's tail, which hung down by his ear. "Oh, no—well, I mean, I know how it is. You run sort of a cat orphanage here. But—"

"Menagerie!" snorted the old man. "Get on with it, boy!"

"Colonel Mace, you can't run cats like a military post," Miss Tabitha snapped.

Though his face was miserable, Sam Bailey said firmly, "Now Miss Tabitha, the town council has voted on it, and as poundmaster I've been ordered to tell you this: your cats have been declared a public nuisance. You must get rid of the cats."

Sarah gasped and sat up straight, staring at the man. No! How could they? No!

"I won't," said Miss Tabitha.

"You will!" exclaimed the colonel.

At this point Alexander jumped down from the chair back, walked deliberately to the couch, and leaped into the colonel's lap. He curled himself up and began licking his tail.

"Really!" Colonel Mace stood up, dumping Alexander to the floor. "Insufferable!"

"You should be honored, sir! It's all right, Alexander."

The cat stalked out of the room.

The old lady turned to Sam Bailey. "Now, Sam,

you know very well I won't get rid of my cats. I'll try to keep them shut up in the stable during mating season, and people needn't—"

"Great Caesar!" the colonel shuddered. "Shut up screeching in a shed next door to *me!*"

"No, ma'am, that wouldn't do. I'm terribly sorry, but the council's order is clear. The cats must go."

"This is my property!" the old lady cried angrily. "I can keep cats if I like!"

Sam Bailey shook his head sadly.

Miss Tabitha's mouth drew in, pinched among the wrinkles. "And if I refuse?"

"I'll have to come and get the cats. Look, Miss Tabitha, if the cats are broken up, they won't run in gangs at night. I'll let you have two weeks to find homes for them. I think probably you could keep three cats." He looked defiantly at the colonel. "But at the end of two weeks if you have more than three left, I'll have to take the rest away."

"And put them to sleep!"

"I'll find homes for them," he soothed.

But Sarah knew as well as Miss Tabitha did that the town wouldn't support a great horde of cats at the pound. If the vet didn't find takers for the cats in a few days he'd have to "put them to sleep"—kill them.

It had happened, the very worst thing Sarah had feared when the men came in looking so official.

She'd tried to hope they'd come only to give a warning about making the cats behave. But no. The cats must go.

She looked to Miss Tabitha, hoping that somehow the old lady could think of something to say that would change things. But everything had been said. She was silently showing the men out the front door. Although the colonel wouldn't unbend enough to smile, he was saying with satisfaction, "Madam, I am right. You know I am!"

Sarah dropped her head against Amarantha's fur because her face was crinkling and sobs were coming. Everything was ruined. They might as well tear down the House of Thirty Cats if they were going to take all the cats away. All the lovely cat-life arrangements—the kitten box behind the stove always full, the cat garden. And the locked room. Now she'd never find out about it. But what about poor Miss Tabitha? She'd been selfish, thinking first of her own loss. It was even worse for Miss Tabitha.

Sarah raised her head and saw the old lady standing in the front room, eyes not seeing.

"I could move to another town," Miss Tabitha said aloud to herself.

But she wouldn't. She'd lived in this little house with its gray stable and old apple trees all her life. It fit around her. Sarah couldn't imagine Miss Tabitha trying to move all her cats to another town, trying to find a neighborhood where people wouldn't object to her cats.

What would she live for now? Her life all shrunken down to three cats. Sarah wondered if that was what the old lady was thinking. She watched the lined face anxiously. What if Miss Tabitha cried? She'd never seen a grown-up cry. It would be awful. She wouldn't know what to do.

Angrily she burst out, "It's all Tarnish's fault!"

If the cats were running wild at night, then he was leading the pack. Trying to make Miss Tabitha forget about crying, Sarah told her of the moonlight night she'd seen Tarnish and the two other cats under her window.

"Yes, Tarnish is gone," Miss Tabitha admitted.

At least he'd disappeared from the sickroom. But, she added wearily, she didn't think he was leading packs. It was just that all the cats were out on the town now that spring was here.

"If we could just keep your cats shut up—" Sarah ventured.

"Colonel Mace would still object." The old voice sounded hopeless.

"I hate that man, so stiff and right!" She couldn't bear for things to be so awful for Miss Tabitha. "If *he'd* go—"

"The town council has voted. Sam Bailey will come for the cats."

So they came back to the finality again. Miss Tabitha had two weeks to get rid of her cats. She began to name over her pets. She'd keep Alexander, of course, and Amarantha. Which would be the third cat? Horace? He had been with her the longest. She'd never be able to give him away, for who'd want a grouchy old cat who slept most of the time? He hadn't much longer to live, anyway. Perhaps the best thing would be to put him to sleep. Sarah thought Miss Tabitha was going to cry then, but her voice straightened and went on. If not Horace, then perhaps she'd keep Felicity. But what about good old Peter, such a faithful friend? And the warriors, Napoleon and Wellington. If they were separated, what would they do without each other to quarrel with? Certainly no one would accept *two* quarreling tomcats. For that matter, who would want gloomy Brumple? And Ladybelle, Cozy, Mr. Tolliver; she couldn't part with them.

Sarah couldn't stand the sound of the miserable voice going on and on.

"Miss Tabitha, Miss Tabitha," she said to get attention. "Look, I'll help you. I'll help you find homes for the cats. We have two weeks. We won't let any of the cats die."

She said she'd heard Mrs. Ritchard, the librarian, say she needed a smart cat to catch the mice in her kitchen. Skittles was such a clever kitten, he should suit her nicely. Mrs. Ritchard would give Skittles a good home, Sarah said, trying to sound cheery.

Miss Tabitha agreed to that. She didn't mind giving kittens away. But she wasn't much cheered. She seemed to be thinking of something else. Sarah had a sudden picture of the old lady taking all her cats into the locked room and simply disappearing.

There was no point in going on with the knitting lesson today. Sarah hunted out Skittles from under the kitchen table and said good-by to Miss Tabitha, setting off to give away the first cat.

Outside a movement made her look at the field grass beyond the yard. There, looking through the tall grass, was the black face of Tarnish. He was watching her. Sarah stood motionless, clutching Skittles. So he wasn't gone, not really gone. What did he want? Why didn't he go on his wandering way, as Miss Tabitha had said he would?

Was he only a poor wild stray, wild only because no one had ever been kind to him? Sarah looked at the yellow eyes staring at her. When Alexander looked at her, his proud eyes seemed to say, "I am Cat, and you are Human, and someday I might sit on your lap if I so choose." But these eyes, this sparking glitter, these were a wild beast's eyes turned on an enemy. The cat's eyes showed nothing of "you-and-I." Tarnish knew nothing but himself. He knew only what he wanted.

The grass waved, and the face was gone. Sarah could move again. She went away, afraid because Tarnish was watching the House of Thirty Cats.

CHAPTER FOUR

Skittles was back. So far she'd given away only one cat, and that had ended in an awful bobble. Mrs. Ritchard had been glad enough to take Skittles because she needed a mouser. But the next night she'd telephoned Sarah to come and get him. When Sarah had gone to her house after supper, Mrs. Ritchard met her at the door, holding the kitten by the scruff of his neck.

"Take this thing away," she said, thrusting Skittles into Sarah's arms. "You should see the mess he's made!"

She didn't offer to let Sarah in, however. She was furious with the cat and included Sarah in the blame. The librarian had no children, and she and her husband were gone to work all day. This evening they'd come home to "a perfect shambles!" Skittles had pulled out a streamer of toilet paper from the bathroom through the hall and into the living room. There he'd played in the paper, shredding it. In the kitchen he'd rummaged in the garbage pail for bones, upsetting the garbage all over the kitchen floor. A sweater she'd been knitting was lying on the sofa, and he'd slept on it, leaving hairs clinging to the wool, and when she and her husband walked in the door, "the little monster" was chasing the unraveled ball of yarn through the coffee grounds and wet garbage on the kitchen floor.

Sarah felt shriveled with shame. If Mrs. Ritchard had yelled it might not have been quite so bad. But the librarian was the kind of person who grows cold in anger. Her voice was precise, and when she called Skittles dirty, it came out "deer-ty", the very sound of distaste for filthiness.

"But what can you expect?" the grown-up concluded. "I should have known better than to take one of Miss Tabitha Henshaw's cats."

With that, she shut the door. Sarah tucked Skittles under her coat, telling him he was really a very lovable kitten. Skittles minded his disgrace not at all. He purred happily and pushed his head out of the top of her jacket to tickle her chin with his whiskers.

A cat screech pierced the dusk of evening, followed by spittings and snarlings. Some of Miss Tabitha's cats? Of course she'd be blamed now even if they weren't. Still, the cats did make horrible sounds. Where was Tarnish? What if he leaped out at her, yellow-eyed and raging? No matter what Miss Tabitha said, Sarah was afraid of Tarnish. She was glad to reach the little white house, though unhappy to report Skittles' failure. Miss Tabitha was simply scornful of the librarian for not appreciating Skittles, and without many further words Sarah left to run the few blocks home.

Through the weekdays that followed she'd asked several children and grown-ups if they wanted a cat and had found no takers. Two days ago she'd emptied her piggy bank and paid for an ad in the newspaper. The ad read: "Free: Fine cats of all colors and ages. Call 5-6202." That was Sarah's telephone number. So far no one had called.

Now it was Saturday, the day set for the Naming of the Cats. Sarah tried to forget all the troubles and enjoy the happy occasion. Outside the weather was wild and stormy for the end of April, with a heavy, gray-smeared sky and wind gusts throwing spatters of rain against the window. It only made Miss Tabitha's kitchen seem cozier, a fire glowing in the cookstove, the room busy with cats. Sarah sat on the rag rug, surrounded by kittens trickling out of the box over the floor. Ladybelle was lying in the kitten box, purring and *prrting* to entice her wandering children back from their explorings that worried her so.

As usual Miss Tabitha had a little duty before they could get on to the important business. She was doctoring Smoke. Smoke was a sad, skinny cat who'd strayed into the yard one rainy day earlier in the spring. He was the color of mouse fur, dull gray with no stripes, and it depressed Sarah to look at him. He looked exactly as she felt on her days of being dullest-gray-Sarah.

The old lady had decided that he was so droopy because he had fur balls. She explained to Sarah that when cats lick themselves, sometimes they swallow their loose hair, and it collects in wads in their stomachs. Then they need a good purging. Holding the cat firmly under her arm, Miss Tabitha scooped up a gob of vaseline onto her finger and smeared it on the roof of the cat's mouth behind his teeth.

"There, Smoke, now you'll be better," she said, releasing the struggling cat out the back door. She told Sarah, "He'll swallow the vaseline to be rid of it, and the grease will act as a strong laxative, scouring out his insides."

At last it was time to name the kittens. Miss Tabitha settled in the rocker by the stove, and she and Sarah began studying the kittens. They could walk without wobbling now. The all-black kitten was off by himself, as usual, investigating the open door to the cellar. Sarah's kitten was cautiously, cautiously stalking him, weaving her small rear in readiness for a pounce, but he ignored her. The white-spotted kitten was having a fight with the edge of the rag rug, and the other black kitten had just nosed up to the straws of the broom and jumped back from the tickle on her nose.

Sarah saved for last the delight of naming her kitten. First and easily came the name for the spotted one. He lay on his back kicking the edge of the rug with his hind legs. He was so funny and fat, a round little Panda bear. Of course, his name must be Hodgepodge, as Sarah had said when she first saw him. Miss Tabitha thought that was just the name for him.

So Sarah tapped the wiggling kitten on his head with her finger, saying, "I name you Hodgepodge."

The long-haired kitten with the white spot under her chin came smoothing against Miss Tabitha's feet. She took the kitten up into her lap and stroked the black fur. Sarah and Miss Tabitha agreed that this little cat should have a sweet name to suit her sweet nature. Responding to the stroking, the kitten purred a ragged little beginner's purr.

"Are you singing to me?" the old lady murmured.

Sarah, watching, cried, "Honeybird!"

"Exactly!" Miss Tabitha rocked happily in her chair. Honeybird purred her satisfaction, too.

Sarah's kitten was stalking her black brother, who wanted to be alone at his explorings. Cornered under the kitchen sink, he turned an angry black face and spat at her, lips pulled back on sharp little teeth.

"He's Lucifer!" exclaimed Miss Tabitha. "The spitting image!" She crickled at her joke. "We haven't had a Lucifer for a long time. Yes, that's who he is."

Now it was time for Sarah's kitten. Sarah watched the little black cat scamper away from Lucifer to bat at the broomstraws, white paws flashing. Then the kitten stopped and sat neatly, staring at the broom, not moving. Who knew what she was thinking? She looked so serious, except for the white stripe on her nose.

"What do you think your name is?" Sarah said to her kitten. "Are you Cat?"

Slowly, slowly, the kitten reached a paw toward the broom—and then darted a scratch at it before the broom could fight back.

"Oh, my little bug." Sarah laughed. "Oh!"

For there it was: Lilybug. A name funny and dear like the kitten, delicacy and humor by turns. It was similar to the mother cat's name, too, Ladybelle, which Sarah liked so much. And when her kitten was grown, if she became a lovely, serene cat, she could be Lily. Sarah told Miss Tabitha, who nodded in approval that Lilybug she was.

Sarah picked up her kitten and cupped it in her hands so they could look into each other's eyes.

"Now, my dear," she said, feeling like a mother, "your name is Lilybug, and you are my little cat."

Lilybug whisked a paw at Sarah's hanging hair, and Sarah held her under her chin.

The kitchen was at peace. Sarah and Miss Tabitha sat each with a kitten while the fire in the stove popped and the rain spattered against the window.

Then the kittens had a special bowl of milk to celebrate their naming. They were just learning to lap, and Hodgepodge had a great deal of trouble with the milk drops on his whiskers. Lilybug's method was to lap with both front paws planted in the bowl. Honeybird was dainty, and Lucifer snubbed the whole business to nurse on his mother.

Leaving the kittens to their refreshments, Sarah and Miss Tabitha moved to the sitting room for another knitting lesson. Alexander came dashing up the cellar stairs, fresh from the outdoors, shaking wetness from his fur. He whirled past them to leap onto the front room chair and look out the window. Sarah thought he wanted out again, but Miss Tabitha shook her head.

"He just wants to see where he's been," she said. "Cats love to look out windows. I think they get a better view of things that way, like a boy looking through a knothole in a fence."

Sarah sat down to her knitting, and today she began to get the feel for holding the needles and pulling the yarn through the loops. She couldn't talk while knitting, though. At the end of the second row of stitches she put down the needles.

"About giving away the cats," she began, "I was thinking. Maybe I could invite some of the girls here after school, and we could have a cat auction. I'll bet they'd have fun bidding on the cats."

She supposed, though, that Miss Tabitha wouldn't want a lot of children in her side yard. She was right. The old lady rustled in her chair and muttered something about "making a circus of the cats." For a moment Sarah was impatient with her. Miss Tabitha wasn't trying to do a thing about meeting the deadline for giving away cats.

"All right, then, what shall we do?" Sarah demanded.

And then she was ashamed, for obviously Miss Tabitha just didn't know what to do, saying in a faint voice, "All I can think of is to try to find nice homes for the cats."

"That Colonel Mace!"

Sarah took up her knitting and finished a whole row, thinking wicked thoughts about the old man with his stern face and bossy-looking hooked nose. She dropped her needles again.

"How could Alexander ever want to sit on his lap! Whatever possessed you, Alexander?" she addressed the tawny gold cat. He looked at her from the chair back, then turned again to the rain-streaming window, keeping his secrets.

"I expect he was teasing the colonel." Miss Tabitha chuckled. "Haven't you noticed that in a roomful of people a cat will always choose to sit in the lap of the person who wants him least? Maybe those are the people who need cats most, and the cats know it."

Sarah had never thought of people *needing* cats. They took cats for pets because they enjoyed cats or they wanted a mouser. Still, Lilybug was more than that to her; she'd needed a cat for a friend. Sarah picked up her knitting and explored the idea. What a lovely world it would be if each person had a cat that was just right for him. A happy cat for a sad person to cheer him up, a scrawny kitten for some plump lady who had no children and wanted to mother something. A woman always flying around nervously might need a cozy cat to hold in her lap, and the cat should have a soothing purr. She imagined a sun-weathered farmer walking in his woodlot with a vigorous tomcat. . . . Good heavens, what kind of cat would Colonel Mace need? For that matter, what kind of cat would fit Mrs. Ritchard? Skittles certainly hadn't suited her.

Suddenly the idea came into full flower, as the Japanese paper flowers open in water. She'd fit cats to people. That's how she'd give Miss Tabitha's cats away. She'd go out and study each person she met to discover what kind of cat that person would need, and then she'd choose a cat from the variety in the House of Thirty Cats.

In excitement she told the idea to Miss Tabitha. The old lady's face glowed. Of course! It was exactly the way to place cats! Then she said doubtfully, "But how will you get the people to accept the cats?"

Sarah hadn't thought of that. Oh, dear. But she refused to be discouraged from her lovely plan.

"I'll figure that out when the time comes."

Sarah begged off from the knitting. She wanted to go down to the library right away to start studying Mrs. Ritchard. After all, it was known that she wanted a cat. So Miss Tabitha, hopeful again, saw her out the door with good wishes.

Sarah huddled her hood over her head and splashed happily through the rain puddles. She felt so busy and alive. She wasn't just wandering aimlessly through wet streets; she had a purpose, a plan to carry out.

Her way to the library passed the butcher shop, and on impulse she turned into the doorway. The

shop was small, but it did a good business, for as Sarah had heard her mother say, the meat was the best in town, and the prices were reasonable. Behind the meat counter display the butcher worked at a cutting table, standing in drifts of sawdust curls on the floor to catch the blood. Mr. Pantiega was short, with black hair and thick red cheeks. Sarah thought of him as The Jolly Butcher.

Mr. Pantiega was cutting up a chicken for a young woman with two little run-around children, and Sarah used the time to study him. He was kind to give scraps to Miss Tabitha for her cats. Maybe he'd like to have a cat. What kind of cat for The Jolly Butcher? She watched him break the chicken joints with quick cracks of his knife. His breath wheezed between his teeth as he concentrated on his work. But none of that told her very much about Mr. Pantiega and what kind of cat he'd need.

Change counted out to the young woman, he turned to Sarah. "What for you, young lady?"

"Oh—oh, I'm just looking."

She giggled. People didn't come into butcher shops "just looking," the way you did in ladies' dress shops. Unless maybe you were a hungry beggar.

Politely she said, "It's awfully nice of you to give scraps for Miss Tabitha's cats," to introduce the idea of cats. "Do you have a cat, Mr. Pantiega?"

"Nope. Your mother send a list with you?"

"I—well, no, I just came in to—to get out of the rain."

The butcher returned to the meat block where he was working on a large piece of bloody meat. Sarah tried again.

"Did you know that Miss Tabitha Henshaw has to get rid of her cats?" She told him about the ultimatum.

"That so? Say now, that's too bad." He looked sorry, but he went on with his meat cutting. "If I hear of anybody wants a cat, I'll tell Miss Tabitha."

She gave up. Mr. Pantiega didn't seem very jolly

today. She'd come back another time to study him some more.

Sarah went out into the rain and walked to the corner. To the right the street led to the library. To the left half a block was Papa's printing shop. Sarah stood thoughtfully in a puddle, watching twigs hurry to the sewer on a stream of water in the gutter. The water swirled wide at the sewer opening, carrying the twigs in a circle in the open air before they rushed on down to underground darkness. Sarah turned left.

Papa was busy helping a girl choose the style of engraving she wanted on her wedding invitations. Sarah went behind the counter and looked at a form of type made up on a slab. She knew better than to touch anything, for mixing up type is one of the worst things you can do in a printing shop. Sarah could read, slowly, the upside-down reversed words. The form she was reading contained something dull about a special sale at one of the stores, to be printed on sheets of paper for boys to stick on car windshields for advertising.

Sarah liked the wedding invitations better, with their lovely scrolly lines. Best of all she treasured the pages that Papa sometimes made up especially for her from children's books. Once on rich parchmentlike paper he'd copied the story from one page of *Cinderella*. He'd used wedding invitation type so that the page of words *looked* like something out of a fairy tale, flowing handwriting script, with tall pointed *t*'s that made her think of spired towers, and elegant swoops for the tails of *p*'s and *y*'s, ladies dipping in curtsies. A page from *Winnie the Pooh* he'd done in fat, funny type that was just like Pooh Bear.

After the bride-to-be left, Sarah chatted a bit with Papa, working up to telling him about the troubles at the House of Thirty Cats, about the ultimatum. She didn't mention her plan, though.

"I'm sorry to hear that," Papa said, his hands busy with bits of type. "Miss Tabitha Henshaw is very good to cats. People ought to leave her alone."

Sarah knew Papa would sympathize. He was kindhearted even if he was absentminded and didn't always know what was going on in the outside world. He didn't know of anyone who wanted a cat, however.

Sarah changed the subject. "Mr. Riley next door. What's he like, Papa?"

Mr. Riley was a tailor. He had a narrow shop with sewing machines and bolts of cloth. Sarah wished that he sat cross-legged on a cushion, flourishing a long thread in the air, the way tailors did in stories. She also wished he were named Monsieur Rattibone or some very proper English name, to fit a tailor.

"He's a quiet man, well-spoken," Papa replied. "We get along. Why?"

"Oh, nothing. Good-by, Papa. I'm going to the library."

Outside the shop she paused to look in the window at Mr. Riley sewing at a machine. Watching him from a distance told her nothing about what kind of cat he'd need.

The rain had let up to a cool dampness in the air. Sarah walked slowly toward the library, her stomach reminding her that she was hungry, that it was almost lunchtime. At last she admitted to herself that she'd been putting off going to the library. When she came right down to thinking about it, she didn't want to study Mrs. Ritchard after all. She kept remembering Mrs. Ritchard's voice saying "deer-ty" and her face so cold, with the smooth dark eyebrows lying against her pale forehead.

However, she'd reached the library. Sarah made herself go up the steps. Several children were hunting books along the shelves in their section, and somebody's mother stood by the adult nonfiction shelves reading a book in her hands. Mrs. Ritchard was typing at her desk, and Miss Jones was nowhere in sight. Sarah chose a volume of an encyclopedia and took it to a reading table near Mrs. Ritchard's desk.

She watched Mrs. Ritchard check out books for

two girls. Her fingers were quick with the cards, she ordered the books in neat stacks, but she didn't talk to the girls. So businesslike and efficient she was. No wonder rambunctious Skittles had been the wrong cat for her. Would *any* cat be right for her? She certainly didn't seem the kind of person who'd like cats. Sarah couldn't imagine the librarian chasing gaily after a kitten or laying her head on a cat's side to feel the purrings.

She was doing things backward, thinking Mrs. Ritchard wouldn't suit a cat. She'd have to find out more about the librarian. She went to Mrs. Ritchard's desk.

"Yes?"

Sarah didn't know what to say. "Um—I liked that book about the big Irish family."

"That's good."

"Um, it was—homey. They all had such good times together."

Mrs. Ritchard said briskly, "Now, Sarah, you can't be lonely for a family. You have a brother and a sister."

"Ye-es, but I'm in the middle."

"Oh, the middle." Mrs. Ritchard's face slowed with a remembering look. "I was a middle child, too. It can be even more lonely than being an only child. Well, Sarah did you want something?"

Sarah fidgeted. She didn't like Mrs. Ritchard to talk about being lonely and the middle child, acting as if she might be like Sarah. Mrs. Ritchard was the one who had said "deer-ty." Still, Sarah tried once more.

"I'm sorry about the cat."

"Hm," said the librarian.

"Would you like for me to put away some books for you?"

"No, thank you, we need trained people for that."

Sarah turned away.

"You might push this cart back into the stacks if you want to help." She pointed the direction.

Sarah steered the cart of books back into the rows of shelves. There she came upon Miss Thelma Jones sitting on a high stool reading a book. She looked a little guilty at being caught reading and slid awkwardly down from the stool, saying she'd take the cart. Under the reading lights the woman's skin had a greasy shine. Her hair hung lank, parted in the middle and held back on each side with a bobby pin. Sarah wondered how Miss Jones could bear to be so plain. Would she need a cat to cheer her up, or what? Sarah considered saying something to pump Miss Jones, but suddenly she felt tired. She simply couldn't think of a thing to say. She nodded and turned to leave.

As she rounded the corner of the bookshelves she looked back. The assistant librarian had picked up the book she'd been reading, and Sarah saw a word on the cover. *Witchcraft.* Miss Thelma Jones, mousy librarian, was reading a book about witchcraft. And in the midst of her plain face her tongue was stuck out between her teeth, flicking back and forth as she read.

So! All the morning's frustrations at understanding people welled up in Sarah. She hurried out of the library as a storm of anger rushed over her. People kept *changing.* She'd think she had them typed, and then they'd twist a little. They'd do something that hinted they were a lot of other things, too, that she hadn't thought of. And something worse. She acknowledged something that had been a growing suspicion all morning: she couldn't learn very much about people just by watching them. Really to know people she had to talk with them, be around them a lot.

And that was all against the way she was made. She liked to take people for the way they made her feel, the way she imagined them from a distance. The assistant librarian was Mouse Miss Jones, who depressed Sarah because she was so drab. Mr. Pantiega was The Jolly Butcher, who made Sarah feel cheery when she went into his shop. People, if they were interesting at all, were characters set around the edge, with Sarah at the center. It was how she reacted to people that mattered, not what people were like inside with all their complications.

I'm just a little girl, she reassured herself. What do I care about knowing—really knowing—all these grown-ups? I can't understand them, anyway. A little girl couldn't. Fitting cats to people is a lovely idea, but it's too hard to make it work. There isn't time to get to know people, anyway, before the deadline. Really, it's not my problem. It's Miss Tabitha's problem to get rid of the cats. She should be doing something about finding homes for the cats. Actually she's so poor it'll be better for her not to have all those cats to support, anyway. Anyway.

The angry self-pitying thoughts kept coming, telling her she was right. Huddled under her hood she ran home through the wet streets to get away from whatever it was that frightened her.

CHAPTER FIVE

Sarah didn't like Sunday breakfast, and she didn't *want* to wear that dress to Sunday school. She wouldn't loan Bets-C a belt, and she muttered when Papa took the funnies first. Usually the silent member of the family, Sarah was very much in evidence this morning.

Mother straightened Sarah's velvet headband and decided Sarah was coming down with something. Sarah didn't look right around the eyes. Sarah stared in the mirror. Her eyes were clouded gray. Below them her face along her cheekbones had a heavy, dumpty look.

"I'm all right," she said, putting the headband back the way she'd had it.

Just because she wasn't going to follow her Plan

after all, fitting cats to people, didn't mean she wasn't going to help old Miss Tabitha. Of course she was going to help. She'd find homes for the cats. Just not that impossible way of getting to know a lot of strangers.

"Why couldn't we take several cats?" she asked her mother. "Two or three cats wouldn't be any more trouble than one."

"One cat is more than enough," Mrs. Rutledge said, her lips tightening at the corners.

Briefly Sarah wondered whether her mother would like Lilybug. What kind of cat would be good for Mother? No, she wasn't going to worry about fitting cats anymore.

"I know!" she said, trying again. "Let's give Great-Aunt Lena a cat for her birthday."

"For heaven's sake, Sarah, don't be silly. You know Aunt Lena has two pet canaries."

Well, she'd think of something. She would.

At Sunday school Mrs. Grimes, the teacher, took up a penny collection for the missionary work with Alaskan Indians. Sarah looked around at the Sunday-clean boys and girls. They ought to be helping somebody at home instead of those way-off Indians. If they really wanted to help somebody in trouble —Sarah went forward and whispered to Mrs. Grimes. Mrs. Grimes shook her head doubtfully but called the class to attention.

"Listen, everyone. Sarah has something to tell you."

She made a mess of telling. She wasn't good at standing up in front of people and telling things.

"Well, there's this old lady, Miss Tabitha Henshaw, you know? She has to get rid of all her cats. They're going to kill her cats."

She tried to put across her idea, that if each child gave a home to a cat or found a home for one, he'd be helping Miss Tabitha Henshaw. Two boys snickered as she talked, and a girl gave her a disgusted look that said, "Oh, why don't you sit down, Sarah Rutledge." The response was:

"We got a cat."

"I'll ask my mom, but I don't think so."

"Our cat's going to have kittens."

"My dad hates cats."

"I might take a cat—I'll let you know at school maybe."

The teacher spoke kindly, "It's nice of you to want to help, Sarah, but—you know—cats—" She shrugged. "Now today's lesson . . ."

Sarah sat down. She'd failed again, of course. She couldn't do anything right. She didn't know why she ever tried to do anything.

Today's lesson was about Christ's story of the servants who were given talents: five to one man, two to another, and one talent to another. The first two servants put their talents to work and doubled them. But the third man buried his talent in the ground, making no use of it. The teacher explained that the word "talent" in the day of Christ referred to a gold piece; though Sarah thought talent, meaning ability, made sense in the story, too. Not that the story made any difference to her. She didn't have even one talent.

After Sunday school Sarah didn't wait for Harry and Bets-C. She walked off, eyes half closed against the brilliant sunlight. But she did see ahead of her the black heap on the grass parking strip. A bundle of rags. No, a pile of black clothes. And white hair. It was Miss Tabitha Henshaw. She was digging dandelion greens. Sarah glanced around to see if anyone was looking before she approached the old lady.

Yes, it was Miss Tabitha Henshaw, out digging up dandelions by strangers' sidewalks on Sunday morning. She moved in a crouch to another dandelion, pulling her half-filled basket after her.

"Hello," Sarah said, looking around again. Did Miss Tabitha have to dig dandelions on Sunday *morning?*

Miss Tabitha's wrinkles drew up in a teasing grin. "Good morning, Sarah-No. Don't look so shocked. I've already been to early church."

"But—"

"Can you think of anything more glorious to do

on Sunday after church than dig in the good dirt for little golden suns?"

Sarah squatted down beside Miss Tabitha. She couldn't help liking the way the old lady put it. She plucked a dandelion to twirl between her fingers as she watched the brown-spotted fingers slice the dandelion knife into the ground and remove the green plant, complete with roots. What would a stew of dandelion greens taste like? Surely the cats wouldn't eat that. She wondered if the old woman was still sneaking around alleys poking in garbage cans. She did hope the scraps and bones she kept bringing helped fill the cats' stewpot enough so that Miss Tabitha wouldn't have to do that anymore.

"Did you decide on a cat for your librarian?" Miss Tabitha was asking, duck-waddling to another dandelion.

"No—I don't know yet." How could she tell that she'd given up her Plan?

As Sarah's silence went on, the old lady looked up at her, the pupils of her eyes closed to slits against the sunlight, eyes large with brownness.

Sarah reached for a change of subject. "Miss Tabitha, why do you dig dandelions along the edges of people's sidewalks? The field next door to your house is full of dandelions."

The field was beautiful now, green starred with yellow.

"Oh, they think I'm crazy. But I might as well do two things at once, get my dandelions and weed people's grass at the same time. Unh." She pulled up another dandelion by the roots, and stopped to rub the yellow head with her finger. "Though I don't know why people hate them so. They're such a cheery flower, and they come free, a gift from the earth."

"You mean—" Sarah stared at her. Why, it wasn't fair. People would look out their windows and say, "There's crazy old Miss Tabitha Henshaw digging dandelions in our grass," and all the time she was doing them a favor.

Fitting cats to people, now that was like Miss Tabitha's dandelion favors, suiting cats to people who needed them even though they didn't know it. No, Sarah's thoughts turned obstinately, maybe that's just being a busybody. Who was she to say someone needed a cat? Not her business. Maybe to some people a cat was as repulsive as a snake. Though it was hard to imagine a person like that.

Just then three boys from her Sunday school class came along. They looked at Sarah and Miss Tabitha all the way past. One boy said loudly, "The fairy girl's found a witch!" and all the boys laughed.

Sarah stood up. Quickly she told Miss Tabitha she had to go home and hardly waited for the old lady's good-by. She cut across the street so as not to follow the boys.

All the way home Sarah fretted at herself. She shouldn't have run away like that. Miss Tabitha might have guessed she was ashamed to be seen with her. But who wants to be known as the friend of a crazy old woman who keeps a million cats and pokes in garbage cans and digs dandelions around town? Ah, what did she care what people thought of her; nobody ever paid any attention to her, anyway. Still, she didn't like to be pointed out as a fool. Oh, what was the matter with her? It was a beautiful day, and she'd just been to church; she should be happy.

"All things bright and beautiful," she sang and heaved a great sigh. The beautiful day just made her more conscious of how pinched-as-a-sour-lemon she felt inside. How could she be happy with all these troubles? In ten days the cats would be taken away and killed. And she couldn't think of anything to do about it. She wasn't good at doing. She wasn't all bouncy and friendly, getting around to know lots of people and what kind of cat they'd need. How could a little girl understand a lot of complicated people?

Fleetingly came a hazy notion of stretching, herself stretching out to people, they stretching to her. Two pools of pancake batter spreading until they ran together. Hastily she blotted out the picture. No. She'd stretch all out of shape. It was impossible.

The discontent stayed muttering below. When she got home, Papa and Mother were just leaving for church, so she had the house to herself for a while. She read the Sunday funnies, tried reading a book that was stupid, and then she sat cross-legged on her bed and practiced knitting. Presently she found she'd dropped a stitch in the last row. She picked at the yarn with her needle, trying to find the loop and hook it on somehow. Her back grew tense and aching with the picky work. Then she lost the rest of the stitches off her other needle.

"Oh—oh—blah!" She threw the whole mess across the room. Hateful knitting.

She ran downstairs, looking for she didn't know what. Everyone was home from church now, and

Mother was in the kitchen broiling steaks, a rare treat in the Rutledge family. For a moment Sarah brightened. Not only did she love steak, but the bones would be wonderful for the cats' stewpot. But—oh, well, maybe she'd take them tomorrow. She didn't want to see Miss Tabitha again today. At dinner she didn't want to talk to anyone, either, and she ignored Bets-C's chatter about people at church.

When dinner was over it was still only midafternoon. Now what to do? Sarah suggested that the family go for a drive in the country to see the spring wildflowers, but her parents wanted to visit a woman in the hospital, and Bets-C and Harry had plans with their friends. Soon Sarah was alone in the house. Even the neighborhood seemed deserted, front yards empty, everyone gone somewhere on a fine Sunday afternoon. Sarah brought her book down to the living room to read but found herself staring off at nothing. Dust motes hung in the sunlight. What a long, slow afternoon, not a sound from anywhere. Sarah couldn't relish the peace as she usually would. Restlessly she walked to the window. Not a thing moving on the streets, the lawns.

"Oh, all right, I will!" Just for something to do.

She went to the kitchen and got the paper sack of steak bones from the refrigerator. Mother knew about the stewpot now and didn't mind Sarah's saving bones. Probably Miss Tabitha wouldn't even be home yet from her dandelion digging. She'd just take the bones over, for the walk, and leave them inside the back porch.

Slowly Sarah walked along through the sun-buzzy sleepiness of the Sunday afternoon streets. The yards were motionless though bright with spring flowers. When she reached the end of the street, however, she saw that Miss Tabitha was at home. Black dress against the greenery, the old lady was working in the cats' garden behind the apple trees. Colonel Mace was at home too, mowing his lawn. It looked so tidy in comparison to the shaggy grass around the little cat-eared house. Bouncer popped through the lilac hedge and ran toward a young peach tree. "Hssst!" The colonel threw a flower stake at the orange cat, who scatted back through the hedge. Sarah could see that Miss Tabitha hadn't noticed, still on her knees in the vegetable garden, back turned to the street. The colonel went on pushing his handmower. Two old people working in their neighboring yards, not speaking to each other.

The colors of the scene grayed slightly. A small cloud had come over the sun. More clouds were gathering on the horizon across the field. Yesterday's rainstorm would be followed by another before morning.

Sarah started toward the backyard, passing Skittles, who was chasing Tansy along the porch railing, the cats' paws running more surely than any tightrope walker's. She stopped to smooth Peter, who was exercising his blunt old claws on an apple tree trunk. Other cats scrambled in the mulberry tree. Such a happy yardful of cats. How bare the yard would seem when they all were gone. How would Miss Tabitha ever stand the difference?

The old lady was squatting between rows of green carrot tops to pull weeds. Mr. Tolliver sat near her. As the cloud passed on, the released sunlight sparkled on his black fur. Sleek as his coat was, he lifted a paw to lick at the white tips. He noticed Sarah first and got up to greet her. His mistress looked around then, but she only nodded and bent again to her weeding.

Sarah said, "I brought some steak bones for the cats."

"Thank you."

"Shall I put them in the kitchen?"

"If you like."

Sarah took the sack into the house and left it on the kitchen counter. She stood on the screened back porch, hesitating, watching the old lady move at her work, trying to get up courage to rejoin her. She didn't know whether the old lady was hurt or angry at her for running away this morning, or whether Miss Tabitha Henshaw had simply lost interest in her. Could friendship wisp away into nothing so easily? A friend . . . Miss Tabitha had been her friend. Sarah recognized it for the first time. She'd been so caught up in the delight of the House of Thirty Cats, the troubles with Tarnish and with people, the Ultimatum, that she'd just been taking Miss Tabitha along with the rest of it. She didn't understand Miss Tabitha Henshaw entirely, didn't even like everything about her. Yet Miss Tabitha had been her friend, a growing closeness circling them together. In this sense, who else was her friend? No one since Kerry left.

Sarah stood among the mops and jars and clutter of the back porch and looked at the old woman pulling weeds in her garden, black cat keeping watch beside her. That was Miss Tabitha, a person she was getting to know, to care for. She wasn't a "crazy old cat lady" who dug dandelions around town. Other people who didn't know her might think of her that way, but she herself had no right. She'd been closer to Miss Tabitha.

Ah, shame. The nasty feeling of shame spread through her body as if it were a real thing in her stomach, along the bones of her arms and legs. Shame, because she'd tried to hold herself apart from a friend, tried to think "I don't really have anything to do with you and your troubles."

Sarah hurried toward Miss Tabitha, meaning to say she was sorry she'd run away this morning, sorry she'd given up the Plan. But it was all so mixed-up to say, and then the old woman looked up at her, and her face was so kind that suddenly Sarah wanted to say, "I love you, Miss Tabitha," and she couldn't say that either, and she burst into tears. Out-loud sobs, tears running down her cheeks.

The old lady didn't put her arms around Sarah and pat her, all motherly, and Sarah was glad. It wasn't that way with her and Miss Tabitha. She got control of her face behind her hands, and presently she felt on her arm the light touch of thin fingers crusted with garden dirt.

"It's all right. Now you'll be Sarah-Yes. Come, help me find all the weeds, the little rascals."

So Sarah knelt between the rows of feathery carrot tops just beginning to peek out of the ground and looked through watery eyes for spikes of grass and straying weeds, fingers reaching into the damp earth. She swiped one last tear from her cheek, leaving a smudge of dirt.

"Miss Tabitha, what will you do?" she cried.

The closeness was still there. Miss Tabitha knew what she meant.

"Do? Same as always, take care of cats," she said cheerily. "Three cats instead of thirty, perhaps, but soon a mother cat will have kittens—and we'll go on."

New kittens, then a stray would wander in. The cat population would build up, and then Miss Tabitha would be in trouble again. In the meantime

Sam Bailey would have to kill all these other good cats.

Sarah confessed. "Miss Tabitha, I can't do it. I don't think I can make my Plan work, fitting cats to people. It's so hard to know what kind of cat they'd need. I mean, so hard to know what people are really like."

"Cats are easier," Miss Tabitha agreed, stopping to tickle Mr. Tolliver's chin with a weed. The cat spatted a sociable paw at the weed, but then he had to tidy up the fur under his chin.

"It was a good idea, though," Miss Tabitha said wistfully after a moment. "I'm too old to get to know a lot of people, but—I thought maybe you could do it. It was a possible good."

Sarah's head drooped more as she pulled at the weeds.

"I read a book over a cat once," the old lady went on thoughtfully. "In it a wise man named Plato, who lived in Greece before Christ's time, said, 'I will never fear or avoid a possible good rather than a certain evil.' "

Sarah looked at her quickly to see if she were being scolded, but Miss Tabitha added, "Don't fret, Sarah Rutledge. I know. I know how hard it is to try out the possible good. Sometimes it's easier not to take a chance and be safe, keep what you've got."

Take a chance. Keep what you've got. Sarah

saw herself again sitting across the street from the house on that first day, worrying that she might lose all the lovely unknownness of the house if she went to the door. But—Sarah shook the soft dirt off the weed roots back to the ground—look how well that had turned out when she'd taken the chance.

Miss Tabitha was going along with her thoughts, too. "Maybe if I'd circulated around town more, I'd have found out I liked people," she was saying. "But"—her expression cheered—"spending my old age with cats hasn't been an evil, either."

Sarah looked at Miss Tabitha. Yes, cats were her only friends. And me, she corrected herself. I'm her friend. For the first time she wondered why this hermit lady bothered with her. Perhaps Miss Tabitha could take one friend at a time.

Sarah turned back to the main problem. "If I can't make the Plan work, what shall we do? Have you found any homes for the cats?"

Miss Tabitha said her milkman might take Cozy.

"Stop fretting, girl. Something will turn up this week. Now, we must plan for Horace's birthday party. It's next Sunday, you know. It will make a nice farewell, too, if some of the cats have to—leave home." Her voice trailed off.

Sarah knew that the old lady didn't really believe she was going to lose all her cats. Maybe she just wouldn't face the idea of the cats being killed because she didn't know what to do about it. Why could she halfway understand Miss Tabitha, Sarah wondered, when it was so hard to know other people? Well, of course she was around Miss Tabitha more. She wouldn't want to be around other people so much—"Oh, *thoo!*" She blew a pent-up sigh through her tongue. Her mind was worn out from thinking around twisting corners.

"What was that little sound you made?" asked Miss Tabitha.

"You mean this?" Sarah curled her tongue into a trough and blew a hooting-fluting note through it.

The old lady laughed. "Do it again!"

"I can even do tunes." Sarah hooted "Yankee Doodle," except for the lowest notes.

So far as she knew no one else knew how to do it, but she'd never asked the other children for fear they'd laugh at her for doing silly baby things.

"Like this?" Miss Tabitha curled up her tongue and blew, but only air came out.

Sarah tried to show her how, but the old lady huffed in vain through her tongue until her false teeth almost flew out. Sarah and Miss Tabitha giggled together in the carrot patch, while Mr. Tolliver looked on with his ears back at such silliness.

Then they planned Horace's birthday. A cat's birthday party would be different, of course. No Japanese lanterns on the lawn or children's party games. And no ribbon around Horace's neck, either.

Horace hated ribbons. You had to think what a cat would like. Mainly Horace liked to eat and sleep. So eating would be the main event, and the party would take place in the yard at dusk, dinnertime. Miss Tabitha said she'd mix canned tuna into a batter and fry fish cakes for all.

"What about a birthday cake?" Sarah asked.

It would be funny to see the old gray tomcat sitting up behind a cake with candles, hissing to blow out the flames.

"Sour cream cookies," Miss Tabitha replied. "Horace does have a sweet tooth, and he loves sour cream cookies."

The party should be more than eating, however. There should be cat games. Miss Tabitha and Sarah decided to hang rubber balls from the bushes for the cats to find and play with. They'd strew around crumpled wads of newspaper that would crackle invitingly when the cats pawed at them.

"And paper sacks!" Miss Tabitha exclaimed. "We'll put open paper sacks all over the yard. Cats love to crawl in to see what's inside and then rattle around in the paper."

A birthday party for cats! There'd be plenty of milk for all the strays that wanted to come. Sarah wondered happily if the word would pass around to all the cats in town: There's a party at the House of Thirty Cats! A birthday party for cats!

It *was* a good day, after all. After the long day

of feeling pinched Sarah felt more open and happy than she had in a long time. It was good to have a friend.

The sun was setting, time to go home. Her throat feeling full as a purr, Sarah said to Miss Tabitha, "Thank you for a wonderful afternoon!"

But as she walked home a thought began to mar her happiness. The birthday party for cats meant the farewell party for the cats. Then—they'd be killed. She wasn't doing anything to stop it. She wasn't doing anything to help her friend.

CHAPTER SIX

A rainstorm came and passed in the night. Sarah woke at first light to the sound of birds singing. The chirpings and calls were as rich in the air as raisins in a fruitcake. A fresh day. Too bad that the cats kept birds away from Miss Tabitha's house. The old lady missed all the bird song. But she must have thought about that possible good and decided she wanted the cats more.

Sarah considered leaving her warm bed and kneeling at the windowsill to watch the birds, but she was too comfortable to move. Her thoughts drifted, halfway between dreaming and the liveness of the bird trills. Possible good . . . that was the lovely thing about imaginings: you could think of so many possibilities. The butterflies that could have been fairies, the house that was special and nearly enchanted. And its locked room that just might possibly be the heart of the specialness of the House of Thirty Cats. And dear old Miss Tabitha, all her possibilities. She wasn't just a set figure at the edge of Sarah's world anymore, not just the Crazy Cat Lady. So—oh, dear, her thoughts were leading her on relentlessly now—there could be possibilities in other people. It would be nice to keep it rather a fairy-tale world, with The Jolly Butcher, Mouse Miss Jones. And yet . . .

A bird in the tree outside seemed to take up the call. "Possible good," he seemed to chirp cheerfully. "Possible good! Possible good!" Sarah lay listening to the bird until she sank back into sleep.

When she woke again she found that the decision was there: she was going to follow her Plan. She was going to set out today to study people. It was a possible good, and it was the only way she could think of to help her friend. She had eight more days. Surely in that time— Now, she wasn't going to worry about how she'd do it, how she'd act around different people. Because that part got too complicated. She'd just talk to people, and maybe things would happen.

On her way to school Sarah figured. Eight more days to give away cats. Miss Tabitha could keep three, and she'd take Lilybug, so that left twenty-six cats to find homes for. Eight into twenty-six went three times and two left over. That meant she had to give away at least three cats a day—goodness! But she squashed down the beginnings of worry. It was a beautiful blue-and-green tree-swaying day, the kind of day for good things to happen.

And at school something good did happen. Lucy wanted a cat. Lucy was the kindhearted girl whom Sarah admired rather from a distance, and Lucy had heard of Sarah's plea for the cats at Sunday school. Lucy had a piano lesson after school today, but tomorrow, she said, she'd like to go with Sarah to Miss Tabitha's to pick out a cat.

A girl from the Sunday school class reported that her mother wouldn't let her have a cat. The only other result of yesterday's attempt came at recess, when one boy called "Here, kitty, kitty" to Sarah. But that stopped as soon as it started, for Sarah wasn't much fun to tease. She only stood blankly, not knowing what to do.

No point in trying to fit a cat to her teacher, for she already had two cats. Sarah put cats out of her mind and tried to concentrate on lessons to keep up with the class.

After school, however, she headed for the public library. Today it was busy with high-school students looking up things for research. Sarah posted herself in front of the shelves in the children's section and pulled out one of her favorite fairy-tale books, *East of the Sun and West of the Moon.* Over the book she watched Mrs. Ritchard. The librarian was speaking firmly to some boys who were busier at noise than studying. Mrs. Ritchard's face was cool, as usual. Sarah had never seen her face soften into a real smile. She wondered if Mrs. Ritchard liked library work.

Sarah was trying to think of something to say to Mrs. Ritchard, when surprisingly the librarian came up to her.

"Sarah, perhaps you can help me after all," she said briskly, though her voice was low with "quiet-in-the-library." "You do know the children's book-shelves fairly well."

She explained that she and Miss Jones were always behind at putting returned books back on the shelves. Sarah might put the children's fiction back, alphabetically by author. She was to place the books horizontally, with spines up, so that they could be told from the rest of the line of books. Then the librarians would go quickly along the shelves later to see whether the books were in the right places.

Sarah realized that Mrs. Ritchard liked things to be just so. Of course a librarian had to keep books orderly; still, it was a little something to know about Mrs. Ritchard. Sarah tried to think quickly, and as she followed the librarian to get the cart of books she asked, "What kind of books do you like to read?"

"I don't have much time for pleasure reading."

At Sarah's surprised look the librarian added briefly that she had to skim through all the new books she bought for the library to see what they were about. "Though I do like to settle down with a good travel book."

Aha. Did that mean the librarian liked to think of far places? It was so hard to know Mrs. Ritchard. Sarah didn't think this woman wanted people to know her.

Left to herself, Sarah began finding the right places on the shelves for the books. It was easy work, and in the process she came upon several books that might be good to read. These she put aside to check out.

"Have you found the magic hole yet?"

The low voice was husky, with golden flecks in it, and Sarah, turning, was startled to find that the lovely voice came from the mousy librarian. Miss Thelma Jones had stopped beside her with another cart of books. She'd heard Miss Jones speak before but not with this personal sound in her voice.

"Hole? You mean for the books?"

"Well, no—*Alice in Wonderland,* I mean, you look like Alice—your long hair and . . ." Her voice retreated to a mumble.

Just the way I do, Sarah recognized, when I say something that turns out to sound silly because people don't understand.

Quickly she said, "Thank you. I'd love to be like Alice. Wouldn't it be wonderful to find the magic hole!"

"You'll find it if anyone ever does." The richness returned to Miss Jones's voice. "From the books you take out I think you like stories that make you dream."

Why, Miss Jones must have been studying her just as she'd studied Miss Jones. Sarah felt uncomfortable to be noticed. Yet she found herself liking the librarian. She remembered the book about witchcraft and asked, "Miss Jones, what kind of books do you like?"

"Oh—books that make me dream, too."

The librarian talked eagerly of books she loved, and they were of all kinds, books of far places and fantasy, poetry and interesting people. Some that she mentioned Sarah had read, and she joined Miss Jones enthusiastically in talking of those. The librarian looked along the shelf and pulled out an old book with a dark cover that Sarah had never noticed.

"Here's one you might like, then."

Sarah opened the book and saw inside the cover an old-fashioned illustration, the only one for the book. It showed a girl with princess-long hair, and she was climbing a dusty winding staircase. Sarah's heart gave a thump. Suddenly she could hardly wait to read the book.

Mrs. Ritchard passed by, glancing at Sarah and Miss Jones, and the assistant librarian moved on with her cart of books.

"Let me know what you think of the book," she said as she left.

Sarah went on with her work. She hadn't said a thing to Miss Jones about cats. She'd forgotten in the fun of talking with her. Well, she'd come back day after tomorrow, and maybe by then she'd have some notion of what kind of cat Miss Jones would need.

Finished with the book shelving, Sarah checked out her books and set off down the street toward the butcher shop. She'd try Mr. Pantiega again. Nice as her visit with Miss Jones had been, she still hadn't given away any of her three-cat quota for today.

The butcher was alone in his shop. Mr. Pantiega, black-haired and red-cheeked, stood behind the meat counter cleaning his fingernails. Sarah had planned her opening.

"Mr. Pantiega, did you find anyone who wants one of Miss Tabitha's cats?"

"Nobody. Sorry."

Sarah sighed. Now what? "Mr. Pantiega—ah—Pantiega— Is your name Italian? Did you live in Italy?"

"Naw. Pantiega, that's Basque."

"Bask?" Sarah repeated blankly. "What's that?"

"Basque," he repeated and then spelled it. "My people are Basque. Live in the mountains between Spain and France. When I was a boy I came to this country to be sheepherder."

He turned to sweeping up old sawdust as if that was all there was to be said. There certainly was more to be said. Sarah had never heard of Basque people before, and here was a real live one right in her own town.

"What are Basque people like? What was it like where you lived?"

Mr. Pantiega was hard to get started. "Good people, work hard, sing. The country—oh, mountains."

Sarah tried to picture it. "Covered with snow, like the Alps?"

"Aw, no. Woods, rocky. Like the mountains of Colorado in this country. That's where I go as a boy. Except that where I go to sheepherd in Colorado it's more dry, more wide-open places than Basque country."

Mr. Pantiega stopped sweeping to stare at the floor as he thought. "Wide places. The wind comes clean, straight, like to blow you out of the saddle. Stars all over you at night, quiet." The words trailed off as he stood thinking.

"You rode a horse, like a cowboy?" Sarah could hardly imagine square Mr. Pantiega loping along on a horse.

"Yeah. Follow the sheep. We moved twice a year, up high in the summer, down to the low valleys in winter."

He poked the broom at Sarah and laughed. "Say, kid, you think those sheep and cattleman wars out West is just for TV and old days? Naw. Still going on. Sheep wreck the grass, make no good grazing for cattle. It's the sheep's feet, see. The hoofs chop up the ground, dig the roots right out. And the way they eat. Eat everything bare."

He stared past Sarah, his eyes looking inward to remember. "I know river valleys out in Colorado where grass was once belly-deep to a horse. Barren now after the sheep, soil won't grow nothing but greasewood, rabbit weeds . . ." He was silent, then added, "Out there, everybody but sheepman hate the sheepherder. Yet you gotta have sheep for wool, meat. I don't like that, nobody liking you. No life for a man with a family, either, gone all the time. My wife, she's got relatives here, so we leave the open places, settle here, sell meat."

As Mr. Pantiega talked, Sarah imagined the faraway "wide-open places" where he'd sat in the saddle, one lone man in the wind. It made her think of the time, one autumn, when she'd gone with Papa to the country to get pumpkins. She'd wandered up the farmer's rocky hill pasture and stood alone in the wind under a gray sky. She remembered the feeling: it had been one of loneliness, yet the wind had cleaned through her. Had it been that way with Mr. Pantiega?

Suddenly Sarah felt she knew Mr. Pantiega, even though at the same time she didn't really know very much about him. But she didn't have to know a lot of details about him to get the feeling of what he was like. He wasn't just The Jolly Butcher. True, he was friendly and jolly at times, but he was a man who'd known other places, other ways of life from that of butcher in a little town. There was a sadness in him, too, that seemed to miss the wide places and the wind.

And a cat for the need? Not a cozy cat, Sarah thought, for he had his cozy life now, with his shop and his family. She thought Mr. Pantiega must need a wide-open-spaces cat.

She smiled at herself. It sounded funny. Still, which cat at Miss Tabitha's was a wide-open-spaces cat? A cat that would roam and then come home, bringing in the smell of cool night air on his fur, a friendly cat for friendly Mr. Pantiega, yet a cat with independence and bounce— Ah. Bouncer! He was the one. Wild, rushing-around Bouncer was the cat for Mr. Pantiega. She realized it with a little regret, for it would have been nice to have placed a mother cat here, perhaps Ladybelle. A butcher shop with all its scraps would be such a good place for a mother cat producing kittens. But Bouncer was the one.

A customer came in the door then, and Sarah was ready to leave.

"Thank you, Mr. Pantiega," she said. "I'll come again."

The afternoon was almost gone, and she should be home soon, so she ran all the way to Miss Tabitha's to tell her the good news. Tomorrow morning she'd take Bouncer to Mr. Pantiega. Sarah was sure that as soon as he saw Bouncer he'd know that here was the cat for him. It was almost dusk when Sarah reached the little house. She saw a light in the kitchen and ran around to the back. Miss Tabitha came tapping to the door at Sarah's knock.

"Bouncer!" Sarah panted from the running. "Bouncer's the one—he's the cat—for Mr. Pantiega!"

She dropped on the floor by the stove to catch her breath, and then she told about Basque Mr. Pantiega and the wide-open-spaces cat.

"Good. Wonderful!" Miss Tabitha applauded. "I can just see Bouncer in the butcher shop, making the sawdust whirl!"

Miss Tabitha thought she should keep Bouncer shut up in the house overnight to make sure he'd be home in the morning when Sarah came for him. If he went roaming tonight he might not come back until the next afternoon. She threw on her cloak and went outdoors to hunt for him, but Sarah stayed behind in the kitchen to visit with

Lilybug. With a forefinger Sarah tickled the round black stomach of her sleeping kitten. Lilybug stretched and rolled over onto her back. Blue eyes opened, and Lilybug gave a scrap of a purr in greeting. But she was so comfortable, so sleepy. Her eyes closed again, the purr straggled back into sleep, and her white paws dropped softly onto her black fur.

"Ah, little puss, little puss," Sarah purred a lullaby.

The fire in the stove purred, too. Tansy was drowsing on the rug, the gold in her fur a brightness against her black coat. The kitchen at dusk was a place of quiet and dreaming. Outside, Miss Tabitha's voice called, "Bouncer? Here, kitty, kitty." Sarah wondered idly if all the cats came pouring across the grass to the old lady whenever she called "kitty, kitty" for one. Miss Tabitha's voice faded toward the stable, and then all was silent except for the *shirring* sound of the flames inside the stove.

In the midst of the silence suddenly Tansy lifted her head. She turned sharply and stared across the kitchen. Sarah looked, but she saw nothing unusual. Tansy often did this, stopping in the midst of play or lifting out of sleep to hark to something. As if the cat were seeing something in the room invisible to humans or listening to some far-off call that spoke only to her. Tansy, in all her beauty of black and gold and wide-slanting ears, was a fey cat, with her quicksilver ways and her listenings. Sarah liked this in Tansy, yet now it made her look nervously over her shoulder. The kitchen was so still. What did Tansy see or hear?

Tansy stared fixedly, ears flicked back. Then with a slipping-smoke movement, she left the kitchen, vanishing up the stairs.

Upstairs was the locked room. Had the Something called her there? Sarah yearned to follow, yet this thing was Tansy's, not hers.

The kittens slept on, the flames in the stove popped, and Sarah waited. The kitchen waited.

Suddenly—a black head.

There, around the open cellar door, Tarnish. The thick head of Tarnish. His yellow eyes glared at her, challenging. Sarah shrank back against the kitten box. Slowly, up from the cellar steps, the black body slid through the opening. Still Sarah could make no sound or motion to stop him. The cat ignored her. With sure feet he walked across the kitchen to the back entry hall, turned, padded up the stairs.

Quick thoughts. Of running to find Miss Tabitha for help. Of Lilybug, who must be protected. Of Tansy alone upstairs, threatened. What to do? Dared she go? She must.

Sarah went to the narrow stairwell that led upward. In fear and yet in something like excitement she tiptoed up the steps. No window, no light. The staircase led upward in darkness. At the turn, in the dark, the stair walls gave the look of closing together, as if to stop her, catch her there. But she came to the turn and the steps mounted on toward the locked room.

As she reached the top her breath came in short little pants, and she kept them soft that Tarnish might not hear her. If he were crouching, waiting in the shadows, his black coat would hide him, but she'd see his eyes. And yet he might very cleverly

close his eyes to hide the gleam, then leap out, slashing . . .

In the hall of closed doors was the faint light of dusk from the window at the front. In the gray darkness Sarah looked carefully along the passage for the cats. Nothing. She put her ear to the door of the locked room and heard only the blood pounding in her ear. No sounds. The cats were in there, and they were making not a sound at what they were doing.

She tried the knob. The door was still locked. Sarah dropped silently to her knees beside the hinged panel. Suddenly she wanted to giggle nervously. Yes, she was like Alice, as Miss Jones had said, kneeling by the little door, looking through to the beautiful garden, too big to go through. Except that there was no magic garden through this door. There was—what?

Sarah put a hot, damp hand against the panel, bent her head to look. The little cat door swung in easily—

"What are you doing?"

Sarah jerked up. It was Miss Tabitha, come so silently. The little woman stood over her, and her eyes were yellow sparks in the darkness.

"I—I was looking—"

"That I see. Have I ever invited you to look?"

She hovered over Sarah. In the darkness, with

her long black cloak thrown around her, her eyes sparking, she seemed like a huffed-up cat.

Frightened, Sarah cried, "Please! Miss Tabitha! Really and truly I thought Tarnish was in there. He *is* in there!" The words tumbled out. "Tansy ran up here, and then Tarnish came from the cellar, and he followed her and—"

Suddenly the cat panel burst upward, and Tarnish flew through it. He was in a panic to get away, as if something inside threatened him. He scrambled past Sarah's knees, leaving a scratch on her leg, and raced down the stairs.

"Lilybug!"

In quick fear for her kitten, Sarah hurtled down the steps. But his tail disappeared down the cellar stairs, and she slammed the door after him.

Then Miss Tabitha came down into the kitchen with Tansy in her arms. The young cat looked unharmed, her golden eyes calm and telling nothing. The old lady's eyes were calm, too, soft and big again, nothing catlike about her now.

"I see you were only trying to protect Tansy," she said gently.

So Miss Tabitha wasn't angry with her. Sarah was relieved, but her head dropped guiltily. She knew she had wanted to see into the mysterious room, too.

Perhaps the old lady understood this, for she said, "The room belongs to the cats. It is their place to be alone and think. There are so many cats here, they need a place to be alone sometimes. A cat finds the room only if he is looking for such a place."

So that was the secret of the locked room. A thinking room for cats. What a lovely thing to be in the world! Sarah had been sure the room was something wondersome. But—was that all of the secret? Why, then, was the room locked? And why was Tarnish afraid? Something in the old lady's eyes forbade Sarah to ask more.

Frustrated, she burst out, "Tarnish shouldn't go there! He shouldn't just roam your house whenever he wants."

Stubbornly Miss Tabitha said, "The room might be good for him. It might bring out the good in him."

"The good! How—he's not—" Sarah spluttered.

Then she stopped. Miss Tabitha Henshaw was determined to believe that Tarnish had some possible good in him. Miss Tabitha was her friend—even if she did seem part cat at times, Sarah thought, her arms prickling—and she didn't want to make her angry again. She wanted to keep Miss Tabitha for a friend.

But *she* didn't have to like that sneaky, slobbery-mouthed cat. Hanging around the house, even going into the wonderful locked room. She'd be watching for him now, and once she caught him in real trouble, then maybe Miss Tabitha would stop standing up for him.

Assured that Bouncer was safely shut up in the cellar woodroom, Sarah hurried home, arguing with herself about Tarnish and Miss Tabitha. The thinking room for cats she saved to wonder about in bed before she slept.

CHAPTER SEVEN

In the early-morning kitchen Sarah finished a bowl of dry cereal. She was up before anyone else, for she had lots to do before school. She needed plenty of time to introduce Bouncer to Mr. Pantiega, and time too to take the orange cat home again if the butcher wouldn't accept him. However, Sarah refused to believe such a thing could happen.

Tiptoeing—she didn't know how much longer Mother would stand for her being gone so much—Sarah left the house. On the way out she cast a regretful glance at her library book. She wished she had time to read more. Last night she'd begun reading the book Miss Jones had given her, *The Princess and the Goblin*. Ah, such a wonderful moment, when the princess had reached the top of the dusty stairs and discovered her great-great-grandmother spinning.

Wistfully Sarah wished that Miss Tabitha's locked room could hold such a mystery. She wanted to believe in the mystery, the possibility of something more. Of course this was just an ordinary little town. Mysterious, magical things couldn't happen here. Wishing she wouldn't, Sarah tested the idea of a mysterious room against the everyday morning light of fresh streets and robins singing in the trees. Probably the room was just a place for cats to be alone, just an ordinary room. And yet the House of Thirty Cats wasn't ordinary. A place with so many cats . . . and cats can't be entirely known, not cats like Tansy, sensing things with her sudden listenings. A room for cats' dreamings . . . The thing was, the room was a place where there *might* be something more. And she wouldn't really know until she'd been in the room.

As Sarah neared the end of the street she saw Colonel Mace in his yard. The contrast between his place and Miss Tabitha's increased as spring flourished with flowers and grass. The cat-eared house and its grounds looked more and more rowdy beside the colonel's neat house with its new paint and straight lines of flowers and sharply edged grass along the walks. Nevertheless Sarah liked the comfortable curve of the cat-tail porch, the green tansy and catnip growing wild at the back, the apple blossoms dropping in carefree fashion on the long grass. Next to all this abundance the colonel's place looked tightly drawn in, as stiffly correct as the old man.

Colonel Mace was marching around his grounds, reviewing his flower beds. A cat must have been there already this morning, for he stopped to straighten the stem of a bent flower. Sarah hoped to slip past unnoticed. But the tall back came erect, and the colonel called to her.

"Little girl. Stop."

He strode across the grass and tapped her on the shoulder with command.

"Now then, I want to know what's being done about these cats. Just as many as ever rampaging through my yard! Isn't that old woman going to get rid of them?" he demanded. "I warn you, they'll all be taken away next Tuesday. What do you say, young lady?"

He seemed to lump her in with the troublesome crew next door. Sarah didn't know what to say. Hateful old man, starting all this misery. She couldn't help it.

"Don't you even care?" she blurted out. "Don't you even care that Miss Tabitha has to get rid of all her cats that she loves?"

Immediately she wished she could vanish. How could she say such a thing to this tall man who frightened her?

"Care? Why should I care about a crazy old woman and a bunch of mangy cats? What does she care about the rights of decent people trying to improve their property?"

No feeling showed in his face. It was as cold and smooth as a snowy field.

Sarah backed away. He *didn't* care, even though she'd secretly hoped . . . But he didn't care. Because he knew he was *right*.

Sarah turned and ran across the wet grass, around to Miss Tabitha's side yard. How could you talk to a man about neighborliness when he was sure he was right? *Was* he right?

Near the back of the house an odd little sound caught her ear, and she hurried around the corner. There she found Miss Tabitha sitting on the back steps with her apron thrown up over her head. She was sobbing in small sighs. Alexander was smoothing against her sides and stretching his nose to sniff at her.

Sarah started to retreat, but the old lady heard her. She wiped her eyes on the apron as she took it down.

"Cozy's gone," her voice quavered. "This morning the milkman took my good gray cozy cat. Gone to her new home."

"Oh, Miss Tabitha." Sarah sat down on the step beside Miss Tabitha and reached out to touch her hand. The old veins stood high under her fingers as she smoothed Miss Tabitha's hand.

"Ah, I'm just a silly old woman. Cozy will be happy on the dairy farm. Just think of all the milk for her next batch of kittens, squirting straight from cow to cat." She tried to laugh, but it was a sad crickle.

"That isn't the worst, though. Look at that. Smell it."

She poked her toe at a lump of hamburger lying on the grass. Sarah bent down and caught a faintly bitter whiff. Maybe it was old. Alexander sniffed at the meat and turned tail on it.

"I found it in the front yard. I think it's poisoned."

"Oh, no!" Sarah drew back from the meat.

"Yes," Miss Tabitha nodded. "I think someone threw it into the yard to poison the cats."

Sarah stared at her in horror. "Have any of the cats eaten it?"

"I don't know." The old lady's voice was a small wail. "Alexander was in the yard—lots of the cats are out—cats get up early."

Miss Tabitha had handled the meat, carrying it back here. It was impossible to tell whether corners had been nibbled.

"Look how Alexander acts." Sarah tried to find encouragement. "See how he turns up his nose at it. Surely the cats are too smart to touch it."

Alexander was upset at his mistress's distress. He wove around her, leaning his golden brown sides against her. Good Alexander. Sarah smoothed her hand down his back, running her hand on up his thick tail as it cocked forward.

"Good Alexander, do be all right!"

"If it's poisoned, if any of them ate it, we'll know before the day's done," Miss Tabitha said. "Poison works fast."

Who could have done such a thing? Anyone who'd poison animals, tempt them with meat that would kill them—! With a sick feeling Sarah remembered Colonel Mace walking in his yard. He was out early. Oh, but surely even the colonel wasn't that bad. Surely an Army colonel would be an honorable man. Yet if he thought he was right, that cats were just pests to be poisoned—oh, no, surely he wouldn't!

Then who? It was frightening to think of some unknown person sneaking around with poisoned meat. It could be almost anyone from the town. People were growing very angry about the packs of cats prowling the town at night. Just last evening at dinner Sarah's mother had reported that everyone was talking of how the cats were running wild, upsetting garbage cans, keeping people awake with their shrieking fights. Mother had frowned about Miss Tabitha's cats, saying sharply, "People just won't stand for such a zoo set loose on the town."

Now someone, perhaps a bird lover, or perhaps only a cat hater, had shown his anger with the poisoned meat.

"We must get rid of it right away," Miss Tabitha said, trying to firm up her shaking voice.

She took the lump of hamburger to the kitchen and burned it in the stove. Sarah wished she could stay all day with poor Miss Tabitha to comfort her. She could help rush a cat to the veterinarian if a cat seemed to be getting sick—if that would do any good. But she had to go to school. And there was Bouncer. At least he was shut up safe from the meat. She went to the cellar and released him from the woodroom.

Bouncer didn't like being shut up, and he wanted his breakfast. He bounded out and wove happy circles around Sarah, then raced up the cellar stairs to greet Miss Tabitha. Before the old lady could worry about parting with him too, Sarah took him away.

As she went out the door she made her voice cheery and called back to Miss Tabitha, "Now, don't you worry. Your cats are much too smart to eat poisoned meat."

And then Sarah didn't have time to worry about poison or Miss Tabitha. For Bouncer didn't *want* to be carried. He didn't want to be taken away from his house, and he wanted his breakfast. The big cat struggled and dug at her arms with hind paws that left scratches. He'd wiggle up out of her arms, then she'd catch him back. Sarah hurried along with her slippery armload, blushing when people on the streets stared and laughed.

And then, naturally, the door to the butcher shop was locked. Mr. Pantiega hadn't opened up yet. She could see him inside, though, stooping down in a corner. Sarah banged on the door and caught Bouncer back as he almost got away.

The butcher opened the door, saying "What's it now?" at the sight of Sarah and the cat.

Bouncer burst out of Sarah's arms into the shop. He ran to a corner, ears back, ready to leap in any direction, alarmed at this unfamiliar place.

Sarah began, "Mr. Pantiega, this is Bouncer. He's one of Miss Tabitha's cats."

"So?"

"Well, I brought him—uh, here, kitty."

She moved toward Bouncer. Frightened, the cat darted away and began running around and around the butcher shop, making the sawdust fly under the chopping block. Finding no way out and growing frantic, he jumped up onto a sink in a back corner of the shop. It was deep, and he fell in, but he scrambled out again before Sarah could catch him. He leaped next to the top of the meat case. And then he saw a fresh side of beef on the chopping block. Breakfast! Bouncer sailed over to the red meat and crouched.

"Hey, what's it with the crazy cat?" cried Mr. Pantiega.

"No, Bouncer! Bad cat!" Sarah snatched him up, though he growled at her, and held him against the floor.

It was a terrible beginning. How was she to convince Mr. Pantiega that here was a cat he'd like to have?

"He's hungry," she apologized.

"Then take him home."

"Meow!" Bouncer cried, struggling under Sarah's hands. He stared up at the butcher in appeal.

Mr. Pantiega looked back at him. "Huh, well, I got something better for a cat. Huh, kitty? Looka here."

He went to the corner where he'd been stooping when Sarah had arrived. He picked up something.

"Hey, kitty, how about this? Fresh caught, still alive!"

In his hand was a mousetrap with a mouse caught in the hinge.

"Oh!" Sarah was sorry even for a mouse.

But mice are for cats. As the butcher opened the trap in front of Bouncer, the cat came to an eager focus on the mouse. Ears popped forward, whiskers fairly sparkled, all of him pointed toward the mouse. The mouse seemed unhurt and ran a little way. Bouncer pounced. But with gentle paws. The play came first.

He tossed it and then pretended not to see. The mouse ran with tail slithering after it. Bouncer caught it back with one paw, let it go again. But this time the mouse got too far. Bouncer raced after it and finally got it after a quick scrabble. Taking the mouse in his mouth, he looked around the shop. Then he ran to the sink in the corner and jumped up into it.

"Hey, some smart cat!" Mr. Pantiega laughed.

Bouncer chased the mouse around the sink, batting it with a paw around the slippery sides. The mouse scrambled up. *Swipe!* Bouncer scraped it down again. The mouse could scamper, but he couldn't get away from the pouncing cat.

"Oh, ho, ho!" Mr. Pantiega roared belly laughs. "What a way to start the day!"

Now was the time.

"Mr. Pantiega, this cat is for you."

"Huh? I don't want a—hey, cat, look out, he's getting away! Ho, what a cat!"

"Mr. Pantiega, they'll kill this cat if somebody doesn't give him a home."

The butcher's chuckles quieted as he watched Bouncer. "Well—"

"He likes to roam, and then he comes home," Sarah urged.

Mr. Pantiega was silent. Then he laughed. "Okay, I'll give him a home. He's a good cat."

"Oh, Mr. Pantiega, thank you! Miss Tabitha will thank you."

Sarah left before he could change his mind. At the door she called back, "Miss Tabitha says to feed him right away so he'll like your place and want to stay."

"Sure, sure," he nodded. He was stroking Bouncer's head.

Now that had turned out perfectly! Sarah hurried down the street in a glow of triumph. She'd actually fitted a cat to a person, and it had turned out right. Her first fitting job! Sarah giggled. She should be a tailor. And that made her think of Mr. Riley, the tailor next door to Papa. She really should go to work on him. Anyway, it was wonderful to see how Mr. Pantiega took to Bouncer. Maybe just now he liked Bouncer because he was funny and smart, but soon, she was sure, he'd see that Bouncer was a wide-open-spaces cat, and he'd take pleasure in that, too. Oh, she did hope that Bouncer was the good and right cat for Mr. Pantiega.

She reached the schoolground just before the bell. Lucy left a group of girls to come over to her.

"Today's the day," Lucy said, smiling. "I can hardly wait."

Sarah had forgotten about Lucy in all that had happened already this morning. The surprise of Lucy's warm smile made Sarah forget too that she didn't know how to laugh and talk with the most popular girl in school.

"Yes!" Sarah laughed and then chanted, " 'Today's the day they give cats away with half a pound of tea'!" The words were from an old song Papa used to sing to her, except that in the song they gave babies away, not cats.

"I don't want any tea," Lucy said and giggled. She put her arm around Sarah. No one ever put an arm around Sarah, not even Mother. Sarah wasn't used to being touched. But all of a sudden a friendly arm was the most wonderful feeling.

Then the bell rang, and they had to go in. Through the opening of school Sarah could still feel the warmth of Lucy's arm where it had been, and there was a little sunny spot inside her that said, "Right after school I'll be with Lucy again."

Presently, however, worry about the poisoned meat began to come back. The day stretched out so long; all sorts of horrible things could be happening at Miss Tabitha's house. If it were Alexander—! She imagined him foaming at the mouth or his golden body all collapsed on the floor. At least Lilybug and the other kittens were safe, she reflected, trying to find comfort. They didn't go outdoors yet. But any of the older cats could have eaten the meat. . . . Sarah worried on through the school day.

At last school was over. Now. Now, Lucy. And now she'd find out if the cats were safe.

Sarah was pleased at the glances the children gave at seeing Lucy walk out of school with her. Mainly, though, she was simply pleased to be with Lucy. Except that now she couldn't think of anything to say. Fortunately friendly talk began flowing out of Lucy right away.

"It's so nice of you to find me a cat, Sarah. I've always wanted one, but my mother said to wait until my little sister was old enough not to pull its tail. But, Sarah, however did you get to know that funny old Miss Tabitha Henshaw? Is she really crazy?"

"No! She's wonderful!"

"She isn't the kind that hands out cookies at the door."

"No, but she's—uh—" Sarah didn't know how to describe Miss Tabitha. "Well, she's awfully good to cats. And she knows just everything about cats."

"If you like her, she must be nice," Lucy said. Lucy was a very tactful girl.

She'd heard that the old lady had to give away her cats—it seemed that everyone in town knew it by the grapevine—so Sarah told her about Colonel Mace's part in the Ultimatum.

"Why, that's mean!" Lucy declared. "It's no business of his if a nice old lady wants to make a home for cats." She patted Sarah's arm. "You're very good to try to help her."

Glowing under approval, Sarah found it easy to

talk to Lucy. She told of the troubles in giving away cats, and immediately Lucy busied her brain with the problem.

"You have to think who'd want a cat. Like new families in town."

There was a new family next door to her, she said. They'd just moved to town and didn't have any pets, probably hadn't tried to move animals. They had children; they'd be just the ones to want a cat to help them settle into their new home. Lucy promised to ask the people.

Wellington and Napoleon. Sarah's mouth went into an elf grin at the idea: if Lucy would take Wellington, and the new family took Napoleon, the two cats could go right on fighting with each other, neighborly enemies.

She wondered which cat Lucy would pick. As Lucy chattered on, Sarah made it a game with herself to guess the right cat ahead of time. Lucy was such a friendly, happy girl, what kind of cat would she like? Roly-poly Hodgepodge? Perhaps the happy Felicity. No, she thought Lucy would want a kitten. She'd bet on Hodgepodge.

Then Sarah began to worry about the poisoned meat and the cats again. She walked faster to hurry Lucy along. At last the girls reached Miss Tabitha's house. Peter was sitting on the front steps, looking at the world, his white fur shining in the afternoon sun. So he was all right. Other cats were playing about the yard, in and under the apple trees. Alexander's yellow coat was nowhere in sight.

"Oh, what a nice cat place!" Lucy cried.

"Yes." Sarah saw Miss Tabitha in the backyard, and she hurried forward.

"The cats," she called. "Are they all right? Where's Alexander?"

The old lady had been bending down to stroke Smoke, the gray cat. As Sarah came running, the slim cat slipped away to hide under a tansy bush. Miss Tabitha's face was tired, but she smiled to reassure Sarah.

"Alexander's fine. Asleep in his chair."

It had been a long day of waiting and watching, but none of the cats had taken sick, she said. It might be too soon to tell, but she thought they'd show signs by now if they'd eaten the poisoned meat. The cats seemed safe.

"Good!" Sarah sighed relief.

"Except Napoleon," Miss Tabitha added unhappily.

Napoleon had disappeared. Miss Tabitha didn't know whether he'd been poisoned and gone off to die. She said she'd thought about it and realized that she hadn't seen Napoleon since Sunday. He might only be out on a long prowl and come back.

Or the warrior cat might have had his last battle, with Tarnish, Sarah thought. Poor Napoleon, poor General Cat.

"Here, kitty, kitty. Here, puss." Lucy was squatting by the tansy bush trying to coax Smoke out.

Sarah had forgotten Lucy. She hurried to introduce her. "This is Lucy. She's come for a cat."

"The best errand in the world, to come for a cat."

The old lady smiled at Lucy, and Lucy smiled back, putting out her hand to shake Miss Tabitha's, not at all as if she thought Miss Tabitha was a crazy old woman. Sarah was glad to see them so friendly. She'd been afraid that Miss Tabitha would do some queer hermitlike thing. But the old lady made Lucy welcome.

Sarah remembered to report that Mr. Pantiega had accepted Bouncer. She told about Bouncer, the mouse, and the butcher shop sink, and Lucy giggled and Miss Tabitha crickled. Then Miss Tabitha led the girls around the yard and into the stable to show Lucy all the cat possibilities. Lucy exclaimed over first one "darling cat" and then another. They went into the house, and Sarah felt a vague worry when Lucy made a fuss over Tansy. Tansy wasn't for Lucy.

"Here's my kitten." She distracted Lucy to Lilybug, who was rattling a marble across the floor. "And here's Hodgepodge."

The spotted kitten was chasing his tail in a vain attempt to catch it and show it who was boss. At

Lucy's approach he rolled onto his back in an invitation to play.

"What a darling little fat tummy!" Lucy cried.

She tickled the round stomach, and Hodgepodge nibbled at her fingers. Lucy laughed, rolling the kitten around. Sarah was about to congratulate herself on guessing right when Lucy stood up.

"There was another cat," she said. "The one I saw first. He was a gray cat under a bush. May I see him again?"

Smoke? Lucy wanted to see the skinny stray, Smoke?

Miss Tabitha led the girls outdoors and called Smoke from under the tansy bush where he still crouched.

"See what a beautiful gray he is?" Lucy said. "Almost a blue-gray."

As the cat came across the grass his fur had a soft shine in the afternoon sun. Now that Sarah took a good look she saw that his fur was no longer dull and matted. So Miss Tabitha's doctoring with the vaseline must have worked. Already Smoke's fur looked much more healthy, as if his innards were in better working order. He was still a long, skinny cat, however, with scared eyes.

Miss Tabitha stroked the cat to keep him there, and Lucy stepped forward, not making any sudden movements.

"Now, puss, good puss," she said gently. "Do you know I like you?"

She reached a slow hand and smoothed his head. Smoke let her, and then he pushed his head into her hand, turning his ears for more smoothing. Lucy sat down on the grass, and the cat allowed himself to be taken into her lap.

"He's going to take lots of fussing over," Lucy said happily. "I'll have to be careful how he's treated at first so he won't be scared away."

"You mean *this* is the cat you want?"

"Oh, yes." Lucy bent her head over Smoke to murmur to him.

"But what's your mother going to say when you come home with a skinny old full-grown cat?"

"She won't care. She said I could pick any cat I wanted since I've had to wait so long for a cat. Besides, he's going to be beautiful when I get him fattened up a little. He's going to need lots of loving too."

Sarah began to understand. Lucy had enough happiness in her to give some to a scared sad cat. She'd take care of him and mother him and enjoy doing it.

"He'll be my blue Smoke," Lucy said, gathering the cat into her arms.

How lovely she made the skinny cat sound. Sarah remembered the times when she'd felt her plainest gray and how she'd thought, "I'm as dull gray as poor old Smoke." If Lucy could like Smoke, if Lucy could see possible beauty in him, then—then! Then maybe she could like a plain-gray Sarah, too. Of course Lucy had lots of friends, but it would be good even to be one of her friends. You couldn't help feeling warm and sunny around her.

Lucy's house lay in a different direction, so Sarah didn't leave with her. As Lucy made her good-bys she added to Sarah's happiness by telling the old lady that she was going to help Sarah find homes for the cats. She watched Lucy walk away, smoothing Smoke as he draped against her shoulder, murmuring softly to him.

Such a nice Lucy, Sarah thought.

CHAPTER EIGHT

Sarah knew she should go home, for the sun was setting. Still, she felt so relaxed and happy here after the long day of worrying whether the cats were poisoned. Now was a time for the treat, a treat she'd been promising herself for some time. Sarah had never watched Miss Tabitha feed all the cats, and she stayed on for the event.

While Miss Tabitha got jugs of powdered milk mix from her ice chest on the porch Sarah played with Lilybug on the kitchen floor.

The kitchen was full of cats eager for supper. Amarantha and Ladybelle wove back and forth around the old lady's skirts, almost tripping her and meowing loudly. "Meow, it's coming," she answered them, but Amarantha talked right on about how hungry she was, "Meow? Meow!" Alexander stood by his own bowl, tail cocked forward, and even he opened his mouth in a lordly "MEOW!" for Miss Tabitha to hurry. Horace came yawning from the sitting room, and Lilybug pulled away from Sarah to plant her front paws in the kitten bowl and look around for something to be poured into it.

The seven bowls were lined up on newspapers along the wall, between the stove and the kitchen table. Miss Tabitha poured into each bowl, emptying the jug. Tansy and Skittles hurried in at the last minute, and the younger kittens gathered, pushing and shoving, around their bowl. The older cats crouched to lap up their suppers, and Sarah laughed to see the line-up of tails. Black tails, gray tails, golden-brown tail, sticking straight out, lying in graceful curves, or waving gently. Although Alexander's body was still, the end of his tail curled first to one side, then to the other, as if the tail tip had a pleasure in the milk all its own.

Two more jugs of milk were ready for the outdoor cats. Sarah carried one and Miss Tabitha took the other, leading the way to the stable. The stable was silver-gray with years of weather, and the slanting roof was spotted with holes where the shingles had blown away. Inside was even more clutter than on the back porch, trunks and boxes, old lanterns, loops of rope, broken tools, a fine place for cats to find cozy corners to hide in.

Felicity rose stretching from her knitted pad in the shadows, but most of the cats came pouring from the outdoors. The sight of Miss Tabitha with a milk jug was the welcome signal for suppertime. Wellington paced beside his bowl, yellow-striped tail jerking. Twenty bowls and pans were set around the stable, and Miss Tabitha managed to fill them all from the two jugs, Sarah helping. There was very little quarreling, though a few cats who got mixed up were hissed away from the wrong bowl by the bowl's owner.

It was the first time Sarah had seen all the outdoor cats in one place, and it was an amazing sight. So many cats gathered in one small shed. Eighteen or twenty cats crouching at their milk, lapping, lapping. The lapping filled the place, a live ripple of sound. For the first time Sarah really understood that thirty cats lived at Miss Tabitha's, not simply many cats with their interesting personalities, but *thirty* cats. No wonder Colonel Mace was having fits, hating cats as he did.

Miss Tabitha took the empty jugs and went back to the house for her own supper. She said she ate only a bowl of cereal and milk, as one should eat lightly in the evening to sleep well. Sarah thought sadly of the old lady eating her meager supper and wondered if she got enough to eat.

Sarah lingered in the dusky stable with the cats. Such a cozy place, she put off leaving. The cats were cleaning up the last drops of milk in their bowls, sitting up to lick their whiskers, yawn, and swipe their tongues at their paws. A few sleepy ones curled up on their pads, but most of the cats slipped out of the stable, dissolving into the dusk.

Felicity came loving up to Sarah, so Sarah sat on a box to take the gray cat into her lap. Felicity turned herself around comfortably under Sarah's smoothing hand. Other cats purred on their pads before they slept. Now purring, purring, sounded in the stable, soothing Sarah to a drowse.

However, it was dark now. Her parents would be worrying about her. Regretfully Sarah unsettled Felicity and stepped out into the night.

Clouds covering the stars brought the sky low and heavy. The darkness had a soft, smothered feeling to it, and a low rumble of thunder rolled in the southwest beyond the field. The wild smell of tansy was strong as Sarah passed the garden and found her way under the apple trees. The stillness held little sounds as the breeze rustled bushes and sent two white apple blossoms drifting down in the darkness. There were movements around her, sensed rather than heard; the sudden gleam of cat eyes startled her.

As she came to the front corner of the house she stopped short behind a bush when she saw dark

shapes on the white porch. Tansy crouched on the windowsill, wide-slanting ears outlined in the dim light from the back sitting room. The gold in her fur caught the faint light, and her eyes were great yellow pools. Below her Skittles stepped slowly backward, a silhouette of arched back and stiff-up tail. And the black shape advancing toward him—Sarah recognized the gaunt body, the slinking tail. It was Tarnish.

Skittles spat and raised a paw, but Tarnish was not interested in fighting with this kit. He knocked him aside with one paw. The black cat lifted on his back legs and uttered a sound to Tansy. Not a meow, but a low note, half question, half enticement. Tansy shrank back against the window.

Sarah knew Tansy was too young for wooing, not yet four months old. What did Tarnish want with her? Sarah was ready to run forward to kick at Tarnish if he tried to harm the lovely Tansy.

But now the black cat turned with his oozing movement and was down the porch steps. Sarah saw more cats in the shadows, hiding under bushes, waiting beside the hedge. The dark yard was alive with cats. None of them seemed to notice or pay attention to her. That darkly crouching cat, that was Mr. Tolliver, the gentleman cat. Sarah wanted to cry out to the cats to chase Tarnish away, but suddenly she was afraid. The day-friendly cats were different in this darkness of night. They too might turn on her.

Where was Alexander? He should be here to challenge the intruder. Or the main warrior of the yard, Wellington, should stop Tarnish. Sarah couldn't see him in the shadows. Oh, where were the strong cats? Already Napoleon was gone. Had that been Tarnish's doing, cutting down his opposition?

Tarnish stopped beside Mr. Tolliver and uttered a short growl. Wouldn't tomcat fight tomcat? No, Mr. Tolliver shrank back. Tarnish ran out to the street, where he cried again, a moan that made Sarah's skin draw up. Then he set off down the street, sunken sides slipping along, tail held low. But there was something different about the black cat's slinking run. Sarah saw how heavy his shoulders were and how they thrust forward with purpose. This was no scared, sneaking cat now. Tarnish was in command.

One by one, shadows slipped out of the yard, the cats followed. Mr. Tolliver, unrecognized shapes, even Tansy. She dropped down from the windowsill, and though Skittles tried to block her way, she hissed at him and ran after the black cat.

"Tansy, no!" Sarah cried, but the black-and-gold kitten was gone.

So it was true. Tarnish was leading the cats in prowling, shrieking packs through the town. Suddenly Sarah understood. Now Tarnish had power.

At night, at least, he was the leader of the cats. And that's what he wanted at the House of Thirty Cats. Power.

Power. This wild wanderer had found a place where many cats were gathered, and he wanted to be Boss Cat. He wanted IN. No wonder he was so sneaky-nice to Miss Tabitha. She was in charge of the house, and he had to win her over. And all Miss Tabitha could see was how pitiful Tarnish was.

Sarah shuddered. Tarnish, his wickedness, seemed to loom over the little white house, a threat to the happiness of the house of cats. Even if it weren't for the Ultimatum, he'd be a threat, trying to take over. It was so frightening that Sarah knew she had to risk Miss Tabitha's anger once more. She must try to make the old lady understand: Tarnish was bad; he must be caught and killed.

CHAPTER NINE

Everywhere Sarah looked there was trouble. She wished she could just go sit under a bush until all the troubles passed away.

There'd been an awful row at her house when she got home that night so late. Mother had said Sarah simply couldn't go to Miss Tabitha's anymore if she couldn't be home before dark. If she was ever late again, that was the end.

And then walking to Miss Tabitha's house after school, she was so nervous her stomach had a loose, queasy feeling. Because how would the cat lady take what she had to say?

The talk didn't turn out quite as badly as Sarah had feared. At least Miss Tabitha didn't turn all huffy-cat. Perhaps she knew that Tarnish was leading her cats away at night. But in the end the old lady was as stubborn as ever.

Her chin shaking but stuck out, she said, "Too many cats will be killed soon. If one cat escapes, then good. Tarnish isn't all bad."

Sarah went away. No point in arguing anymore. She herself would have to do it, anyway. She walked down the street slowly, imagining it even though she shrank from the pictures. Next time she saw Tarnish she'd throw her coat over him and take him to Sam Bailey. The veterinarian would kill Tarnish. And she just wouldn't tell Miss Tabitha.

That day on the way home Sarah looked for Tarnish. In the days that followed she hunted in the alleys and in the field for him. But now she couldn't find him. It was as if he were slyly keeping out of her way. Yet other people saw him. People talked angrily of an ugly black cat jumping at babies set out to sun in their backyards, a black cat screeching on fences, rummaging in tipped-over garbage cans, attacking pet kittens. Sometimes other marauding cats were with him, and people assumed that the whole pack belonged to Miss Tabitha Henshaw. No more poisoned meat was thrown into her yard, but twice boys threw rocks at her house as they ran past. Of course some cat lovers stood up for Miss Tabitha, but the whole town was talking about the wickedness of the cats this spring.

So the hurrying days ran toward Horace's birthday party Sunday night, the sad-gay last farewell for the cats. And so the Tuesday after, the day for killing the cats, came racing forward. Six more days, five more days to give away cats. Bouncer, Smoke, Cozy were gone, Napoleon had disappeared, Miss Tabitha could keep three cats, and Sarah was to have Lilybug. That left twenty-two cats.

Despite the bad reputation of Miss Tabitha's cats, there were still some sensible folk in town who'd give them a chance. Lucy was a cheerful help to Sarah. Sure enough, the family next door to Lucy wanted a kitten, and the children chose Hodge-podge. As the spotted kitten was still a bit young to leave home, they promised to come back for him Tuesday morning, just before the deadline. Lucy also turned up a farmer friend of her parents who needed a good mouser for his barn. He took one of the outdoor cats.

Some of the children at school jeered when they saw Sarah talking to Lucy, "Look at the cat girls!" But Lucy went right on being friends with Sarah. One day Sarah's heart was so grateful, she just went ahead and did it. She hugged Lucy.

Lucy didn't worry about trying to fit cats to people's personalities. She just tried to think who'd want a cat. Her approach reminded Sarah of the young bride who'd been choosing wedding invitations in Papa's shop. She telephoned the girl, and the girl was so nice on the phone that it wasn't as hard to ask a stranger as Sarah had feared. Yes, she *did* want a cat. She loved the idea of having a cat to help her and her young man start out married life. The bride-to-be specified that she wanted a mother cat, and Miss Tabitha found a nice gray tabby in the stable for her.

Still, Sarah kept trying to match the right cat to the right person. One day she was tested.

She had stopped in at Papa's shop and found him next door having a cup of coffee and a doughnut with Mr. Riley, the tailor. Mr. Riley kept coffee on a hot plate in the back of his narrow shop. It was a good opportunity, and Papa helped Sarah by introducing the subject.

"My little girl's in the cat business."

Mr. Riley smiled at her. "How's that?"

"You've heard of the troubles with Miss Tabitha Henshaw's cats," Papa said. "Town council decided the old lady has to cut down the population at her house."

"Guess I heard some silly talk about wild cats."

"Well, Sarah's been helping Miss Tabitha give away her cats."

Mr. Riley finished his doughnut and neatly spotted the crumbs off his vest with a wetted fingertip. He licked the bigger crumbs from his finger.

"Have a doughnut." He offered a chocolate-iced one to Sarah, who took it gratefully, for she loved doughnuts. "Thirty cats, I hear she's got. Now tell me, Sarah, how do you go about giving away thirty cats?"

"So far we've given away only six," she said. "I try—well, I've been trying—" She looked to Papa for encouragement. She hadn't even told him this yet. "I try to suit cats to people. I try to figure out what kind of a cat a person would need."

Mr. Riley laughed. "A tailoring job, eh? Do you guess right?" he asked curiously. "Say, what kind of tailoring job would you do for a tailor?"

Hope flared. "Mr. Riley, would you really take a cat?"

"Oh, I don't know, Sarah. I'm only joking."

She persisted. "But if I picked just the right cat for you?"

"Mm, now." The humor of the idea seemed to appeal to him, for he looked up from another crumb inspection of his vest and chuckled. "I'd like to see what kind of cat you think I need. Tell you what, Sarah, we'll make it a test. You bring back a cat that's just right for me. If I'm suited, I'll keep it. But if you've missed the button, I won't."

"Oh, that's wonderful, Mr. Riley!"

Papa smoothed Sarah's hair, pleased at her delight.

But—she didn't know anything about Mr. Riley. How could she know what kind of cat he'd need? Sarah busied her mind. Mr. Riley was a tailor, and Papa said he was "well-spoken," whatever that meant. Now let's see, Papa liked Mr. Riley, and Papa was a quiet man. He wouldn't like a really rowdy man, so Mr. Riley must be a fairly quiet man too. Well, not really silent, for he was friendly and talkative enough now. Then, say he's a gentleman.

Sarah stood so still, thinking, that Mr. Riley nudged Papa.

"I think she's casting a spell on me," he said.

Sarah looked around the shop for more clues. Bolts of cloth hung neatly on rollers, covered with plastic sheets to keep off the dust. The floor was clean-swept, not sprinkled with threads, pins, and snips of cloth as you might expect. At his sewing machine toward the back, his work was laid out—black wool, scissors, pin-cushion, but not in a clutter. It seemed that Mr. Riley was a very neat man.

"Do you have a family, Mr. Riley?" Sarah asked.

"No, my wife's been dead these six years."

"Oh, I'm sorry."

"Thank you. I make out all right, batching it."

Papa urged gently, "Better go get the cat, Sarah. Remember, you have to be home before dark."

Mr. Riley was chuckling again at his joke. "That's pretty good. A tailoring job for a tailor."

Sarah left reluctantly, for she had so little to go on. How to suit a cat to a man she hardly knew? But how nice for Mr. Riley if she could find a cat he'd like. Poor man, all along, batching it. He needed a cat for company. Not a dog or a noisy bird, but a nice cat to keep him company in his shop. Sarah ran over the list of cats in her mind: Skittles, Tansy, Felicity, Wellington, Mr. Tolliver, Peter—Peter?—the stable cats.

What kind of cat would she need if she were Mr. Riley? Sarah imagined herself an oldish tailor, no wife or children. She imagined herself sweeping the shop every evening, picking up pins (see a pin and pick it up, and all the day you'll have good luck), carefully cutting on wool for suits, measuring men, speaking kindly to people, leading an orderly life.

She thought of all the cats that wouldn't do if she were Mr. Riley. Not Skittles, nor Wellington, not—

She saw the tailor again in her mind, spotting the crumbs off his vest.

And then she reached the House of Thirty Cats, and she told Miss Tabitha all about it, and she picked out just the right cat for Mr. Riley.

She ran all the way back to the shop, and the cat was very nice about being jolted along.

"There!" she said breathlessly, setting the cat down on the shop floor. Now, please let Mr. Riley recognize that here was the right cat for him!

For here was Mr. Tolliver. Mr. Tolliver, the gentleman cat, was for Mr. Riley, the gentleman tailor. He was a polite cat with a nice meow—if only he hadn't started to get wild, following Tarnish—his black hairs wouldn't show up on the tailoring cloth, and to top it off, Mr. Tolliver began to lick his shining vest.

"So that's the cat you think I need," Mr. Riley said. He looked at the small-sized cat sitting on the floor polishing his fur. The tailor laughed. "A tuxedo cat, eh? Black with white feet."

"He's called Mr. Tolliver. He's a gentleman," Sarah began.

But Mr. Riley said, "No, let me find out about him." He bent down to the black cat. "Well, puss?"

Mr. Tolliver stopped licking. "Meow?"

The man put out his hand, and the cat, still sitting, stretched his chin to rub it against the hand, murmuring a quiet purr.

"Let's see how he behaves," said Mr. Riley.

He put some coffee cream in a clean cup and placed it on the floor by Mr. Tolliver. The cat lapped at the cream politely, not spilling a drop on the floor, but he wasn't greedy. After a few laps of his pink tongue, Mr. Tolliver stepped around the shop on his white feet, investigating, sniffing at a clothes dummy, touching his nose to the sewing machine stand. Lightly he jumped to a counter where some rolls of cloth were laid out. Sarah hoped he wouldn't curl up on the cloth. But Mr. Tolliver dropped to the floor again. He walked to the front window case, in which drapes of wool and pictures of suits were displayed. The black cat stepped carefully around the displays and, turning himself around to get comfortable, curled up in the sunlight coming through the plate glass window.

"Settled down just like he's part of the display," Papa laughed.

Sarah looked anxiously at the tailor. "What do you think of Mr. Tolliver? Does he suit you?"

Mr. Riley smiled. "Sarah, I'm flattered. That's a well-mannered cat."

"Then you'll take him?"

Mr. Riley chuckled, smoothing his hand down the sides of his jacket. "Who am I to disturb a cat asleep in the sun?"

So Sarah passed the test. One more cat was given away, and an especially happy suiting job it was. It pleased Sarah to think of Mr. Riley and Mr. Tolliver taking up life together, gentleman cat and solitary tailor.

The next day a small trouble developed, however. Cozy found her way all the distance from the dairy farm, and the bride's tabby came home, too.

Sarah scolded them, "How do you expect us to keep you from getting killed Tuesday if you won't stay at your new homes?"

However, Miss Tabitha said to let the cats stay for Horace's birthday party. Then they could be returned.

Bouncer, too, roamed back to visit Miss Tabitha several times, but he always returned to the butcher shop, where the Pantiega family lived in the back.

When Sarah stopped in for some hamburger for her mother, Mr. Pantiega bragged about Bouncer. "Smartest cat I ever saw. At night I hear him slapping a mouse around in the shop sink. And every morning he's got two mice laid out, one for him, one for me. We gonna run out of mice, I think."

And so the days hurried toward Horace's party. Happy as Sarah was to find homes for the cats, to succeed in matching them to people, it was still misery to see the population at the House of Thirty Cats shrinking. Miss Tabitha became more and more silent as her cats left home, and her crickling laugh was seldom heard.

The cats, too, seemed to miss their friends. Old Peter wandered around and around the yard, in and out of the stable, sniffing at sunny corners, hunting for Cozy until, to his joy, she came back. He showed his delight by licking her thoroughly, and then the two curled up against each other in the sun on the back steps. Wellington didn't seem to know what to do with himself without Napoleon to fight. The yellow-striped tom crouched in an anxious ball under bushes, on the back fence, looking, looking, never relaxing.

The plans for the party were exciting, and in a way Sarah could hardly wait for Sunday night. Yet there was a sadness to the planning, for Horace's twelfth birthday would probably be his last. And after it, the cats would be killed. One time Sarah found Miss Tabitha crying over the stewpot as she stirred it. "Poor old Horace," she'd murmured, but both she and Sarah pretended that her tears were because she'd been slicing onions into the pot.

Still, Miss Tabitha insisted that Horace's party was to be gay, a last big hoo-rah for the cats. Saturday morning Sarah arrived loaded down with things for the cat games in the yard—rubber balls, paper sacks, and newspapers to make crackly crumples for the cats to chase. She also brought two cans of tuna. Miss Tabitha would make the fish cake batter tomorrow, but this morning she and Sarah made the sour cream cookies, Horace's "birthday cake." The baking smell brought Horace nosing out to the kitchen, stretching his stiff old legs.

"No, no," Sarah said with a laugh, scratching him behind an ear. "You have to wait till tomorrow for your birthday cake."

Horace shook his ear away from her hand and sat down grumpily in front of the stove. He smelled cookies right now!

Sarah left then to go downtown, knowing very well that Miss Tabitha would give the old gray cat an early cookie. Sarah had two errands. For one thing, she wanted to return the wonderful library book about the princess, and for another, she wanted to buy Horace's birthday present. At the grocery store she chose a can of sardines. Then she proceeded to the library.

Miss Thelma Jones was up on the reserved-books balcony. While Sarah waited for her to come down, she watched Mrs. Ritchard typing at her desk. It was really a shame that she couldn't think what kind of cat Mrs. Ritchard would accept, after the librarian had said in the first place that she wanted a mouser. Sarah tried once more to figure out Mrs. Ritchard. But that was the trouble: the librarian just wasn't much fun to figure out. Poor woman. She wasn't much fun at all.

Nevertheless Sarah tried. What was it she'd done when Mr. Riley had tested her? First she'd looked out at him, watched to learn everything she could about him. Then she'd looked inside herself to see how she'd feel if she were like the tailor. Mrs. Ritchard had said she was a middle child, just as Sarah was, and that she had been lonely. . . . Now what cat would I need, Sarah thought, if I were Mrs. Ritchard? Fussy about "deer-ty" things, very orderly—me, orderly! Sarah laughed in the midst of the seriousness, remembering the looks of her room. But I'm not much fun, not much happiness in me. Sarah saw herself as Mrs. Ritchard, quick-fingered but rather cold and empty.

I'd want a cat to warm me, a cat with happiness.

And of course the cat would be Felicity, the little purring cat whose name meant happiness. Ah, the very right cat, Sarah knew, for Felicity was neat and quiet, too; she wouldn't offend Mrs. Ritchard's sense of orderliness.

Miss Jones was approaching, and Sarah beamed at her, full of satisfaction. Tomorrow afternoon before the birthday party she'd take Felicity to Mrs. Ritchard's house and simply see if Mrs. Ritchard knew that Felicity was her cat.

"You're looking very happy," Miss Jones said, the warm notes in her voice for Sarah.

"I am. So many good things!" Sarah remembered the book in her hand. "Miss Jones, this is the best book I ever read! But the very best part was where the princess went up the stairs and found—"

"I know. I'll never forget the feeling it gave me."

Sarah and Miss Jones smiled at each other, happy in the sharing.

"Another good thing is Horace's birthday party tomorrow," Sarah went on. She told Miss Jones all about the open paper sacks for exploring, the fish cakes and the sour cream cookies—the wonderful birthday party for cats.

"What a perfectly lovely idea!" Miss Jones exclaimed. "I'd love to see the party. You must tell me all about it afterwards."

"Oh! Miss Jones, Miss Jones"—Sarah forgot to whisper, the words tumbling out as the idea unfolded—"why don't you come to Horace's party? You could see it all. And then, Miss Jones, if you'd like a cat, you could pick out one!"

"I? A cat?" Miss Jones laughed softly. "You know, Sarah, I just might do that. Anyway I'd love to come to Horace's party."

Sarah told her to come at dusk and left, hardly touching the library steps in her light-footedness! All of a sudden how wonderful everything was! Not only the party to come and the idea of Felicity for Mrs. Ritchard, but now how much she liked Miss Jones. There were the feelings they shared, the same likes in books and imaginings about maybe-magic. She wasn't Mouse Miss Jones, for she had all kind of possibilities. Plain face, perhaps, but a gold-specked voice and a gold-specked—what? Sarah hunted for the word. Well, a gold-specked inside. So much more of a person to enjoy now that Sarah was getting to know her.

For that matter, it was something like that with nice Mr. Riley. And with Mr. Pantiega. Now that she knew him better, and about his being Basque and once a sheepherder and all, he was more of a person to enjoy knowing than when he was only The Jolly Butcher. Even if people were complicated, there were all the lovely possibilities in them.

Sarah remembered back to Miss Tabitha's possible good. When she'd decided to follow her plan of suiting cats to people, she'd only been hoping for the possible good of finding homes for the cats. But now here was a bonus: she'd found some people to like. What a good thing she'd taken the chance!

CHAPTER TEN

Mine, thought Horace. All for me. Horace sat up proudly in the grass and surveyed his party with satisfaction. Of course all this excitement was just for him. The nose-tickly smells of hot fish and sweet cookies, the woman making a fuss over him, cats dashing about like sillies. All because *Horace was wonderful*. Of course. A ripple of pleasure ran along his whiskers, twitching them. His throat felt warm and relaxed. Horace gazed at the party and honored it with a rare, rumbling purr. He even switched his tail tolerantly for the young things to pounce at. Though when small teeth nipped, he turned with a warning growl that sent them scampering. Bold young creatures!

He sat tall as long as he could, the king, but his

old legs were tired. He'd batted at one of those round things hanging so strangely from a bush, and he'd run in a sudden spurt after a paper that had rustled over the grass. Gradually he eased his legs down and tucked his front paws under his chest—whoever else had such a handsome fur chest? The woman brought another sweet and teased it against his whiskers. Horace gnawed at it halfheartedly and hissed at a kitten who came sniffing up. But really, he'd eaten several cookies, and he was so sleepy. His eyes went to slits and closed, his head drooped. Nose resting on his birthday cookie, the old cat dozed.

The kitten put a sly paw out at Horace's cookie again, but Alexander came along and growled at the kitten, then skylarked across the grass, chasing after it. Ladybelle's kittens had been brought outdoors for the first time, and they hardly knew what to do about the grass. They touched their paws to the strange stuff gingerly, lifting feet at the prickle. But soon Lucifer found a paper sack to crawl into, and Lilybug pounced at the wonderful rustle he was making. The kittens ran eagerly to meet all the strange new cats, too. With trust Hodgepodge trotted right up to Wellington, who smacked him sharply. So Hodgepodge chased after Alexander. Alexander sprang up the mulberry tree, leaving the spotted kitten to grapple in vain at the trunk with his snippets of claws.

Slender black Ladybelle ran first after one kitten then another, trying to round up her children. Amarantha entered into the fun long enough to chase a paper wad over the grass, then settled with Peter on the back steps to chaperone the party.

Sarah had her parents' permission to stay out later for the great event, and she sat on the steps beside the old cats, watching happily. The yard was popping with birthday-party-for-cats. Ah, the skitterings and the scamperings! Cats up and down trees, cats stalking paper bags, cats battling spools hanging from bushes, cats crouching over birthday cookies. It was too bad that Felicity wasn't there to enjoy the party, yet it was for the best.

When Sarah had arrived with Felicity, Mrs. Ritchard was sitting alone in her house. (Her husband was out playing golf, she said.) At the door Sarah had said only that here was a good mouser. She'd put Felicity down, and the gray cat had walked into the living room and sat down in the middle of the floor. She didn't go worriedly exploring the strange room, she didn't trouble the knitting yarn on the couch, she didn't rub eagerly against Mrs. Ritchard's legs. Felicity simply sat there, tail neatly curved around her white paws, looking up at Mrs. Ritchard, waiting.

"But I don't—" Mrs. Ritchard had said.

Felicity had waited.

"Really, Sarah, you shouldn't—"

Felicity looked at her.

Mrs. Ritchard put out her hand tentatively and patted the cat's head as if she weren't used to stroking cats. Then she ran her hand down the gray fur. Felicity purred. She didn't move, only purred, looking up at Mrs. Ritchard. But her purr was rich with contentment.

"She seems a well-behaved cat," the librarian had said. "I could try her."

And that had been the way of it. Mrs. Ritchard hadn't burst into tears of joy at finding a cat to warm her heart. Nor had Felicity snuggled happily up to her new mistress. When Sarah had left them, Mrs. Ritchard was running her hand over the gray fur again, learning how to stroke a cat, and Felicity was purring gently, the happiness in her ready.

Sarah's kitten came running by, and she caught it up into her lap. When she tickled Lilybug's nose with the tip of her black tail, the kitten caught at the tail with eager paws and bit it, then squeaked when it hurt. Sarah giggled at the foolish cat. She couldn't imagine Mrs. Ritchard ever playing with a cat like this. Still, the librarian might have her own quiet happy times with Felicity. After all not everyone was alike. She, Sarah, didn't expect ever to feel as close to Mrs. Ritchard as she did to Miss Jones. The librarians were simply two different people.

Sarah began to worry that Miss Jones wasn't

going to come. Already Miss Tabitha had gone to the kitchen to ready the fried fish cakes for the cats' birthday supper. The sun had set, and the softness of early evening had come, the time when cats most love to play out. In the fading rosy light when grass shows vivid green, Sarah watched the younger cats playing hide-and-pounce under the lilac hedge. She studied the cats, playing the game of which-cat-will-Miss-Jones-choose? She was sure that Miss Jones would want a cat. It was just a wonder that she didn't already have a cat, for she was a cat-type person. Which cat? Skittles? Honeybird? Wellington? Sarah knew which cat Miss Jones would want. Really, she must have known for some time.

And, ah, there came Miss Jones. How plain she looked, even more so than in the library, where she faded in with the bookshelves. Her body was dumpy in that old suit that pulled too tight. But her face was eager as she hurried into the yard, and Sarah ran out to meet her.

Miss Jones looked at the yard full of cats and exclaimed softly, "Oh, I never! I never saw such a party!"

She stood quietly at one side, careful not to startle the cats, realizing she was a stranger to them. Sarah stood with her, pointing out her kitten and Horace, the birthday cat. Underneath, Sarah began to worry again as to how Miss Tabitha would treat Miss Jones. She'd invited the librarian without thinking about the cat lady's hermit ways. Sure enough, when she'd asked the old lady if a guest could come to the party, Miss Tabitha had said sharply that the party was for the cats, not for strangers to come gawking. However, Sarah had said that Miss Jones might take a cat, and really Miss Jones was very nice. And at last Miss Tabitha had softened enough to say, "Oh, well, I suppose it's a possible good. Let your woman come."

Miss Tabitha came out the back door with a tray of fish cakes. Sarah led Miss Jones to the backyard and made the introductions.

The librarian said to Miss Tabitha, "I'd offer to help with the fish, but I suppose I might frighten the cats. They might not relish their treat coming from a stranger."

"Humph. I guess you know cats," the old lady said grudgingly. "Yes, best you wait here by the steps. Once the cats have their fish they won't care who's here."

So Sarah carried the tray of steaming hot fish cakes while Miss Tabitha dealt them out to the cats. The first patty went to Horace, of course, who woke up eagerly at the smell of fish under his nose. Then the rest of the cats came crowding around to the smell, trying to climb up Miss Tabitha's skirts. Soon every cat crouched greedily over his patty. Alexander and Wellington got into a fight over a fish cake and had to be separated. Alexander was put into the house and Wellington in the stable. In the course of the quarrel each cat had proclaimed his rights in a rather loud voice. The shrieks must have penetrated to Colonel Mace, for the old man appeared at an opening in the lilac hedge.

"Outrage!" he cried, his face pinched with anger. "It's an outrage when a man can't even have a peaceful Sunday afternoon! This zoo—this circus—"

"It's a party, something you wouldn't understand," Miss Tabitha said tartly.

He overrode her. "All afternoon I have been forced to sit on the opposite side of my house wearing earplugs. Now I am going out to dinner. If this—this hullabaloo is still going on when I return, I shall go to the police!"

"Go, and good riddance!" snapped Miss Tabitha.

Sarah had retreated to Miss Jones's side.

"So that's the man who's making the trouble," the librarian said. "Selfish old thing!"

Sarah looked up at Miss Jones in surprise and gratitude. That's what she'd thought of Colonel Mace, but then she was only a child. It was interesting to hear an adult say the same thing, right out loud.

Miss Tabitha huffed around the yard a bit after Colonel Mace stalked down the street, but gradually she settled her feathers.

"What do you think of my cats, miss?" she demanded of Miss Jones.

"Delightful. I wish I had a yard so I could fill it with cats, like this."

Miss Tabitha smiled in satisfaction.

The librarian sighed. "I wish—but my landlady—oh, fiddle, she'll just have to put up with it. I must have a cat!"

"And I know just the one!" Sarah said. "You've picked the one you want, haven't you?"

"Yes," Miss Jones admitted. "That—"

"Wait. Let me! Let me see if I guessed which one you'd want."

Sarah ran across the grass to the cat licking her chest fur after eating her fish cake. Sarah picked up the black-and-gold cat. She put Tansy in Miss Jones's arms.

Miss Jones laughed as she settled the cat against her shoulder.

"You know me better than I suspected, Sarah Rutledge. This is the cat."

Sarah nodded, not at all surprised. Of course Tansy was the cat. Beautiful Tansy for plain Miss Thelma Jones, fey listening Tansy for fey Miss Jones who read about witchcraft and turned ideas around to look at them.

And then crept in the fey time of the party, when the cats drew into themselves in their very catness, humans forgotten. Dusk filled the air, thickening it with grayness, and the sweet smell of the lilacs pierced as the dark came on. A cat moved in a tree, and white apple blossoms drifted down, ghosts of flowers. White Oriole flowed across the grass, silent ghost of cat. Under the lilac cats were sudden streaks of motion, hunting, pouncing, startling. Bouncer appeared, perhaps from hunting in the field, for he had a mouse. As the moon rose full, Bouncer danced with his mouse. Horace watched with wide yellow eyes, Tansy watched, the cats crouched and watched as cat danced with mouse. High in the moonlight tossed the mouse, cat leaping up for it with long flinging legs. Higher, higher, flinging, dancing in the moonlight . . .

And there was a shriek. A cry of pain rang out.

Tarnish had come to the party.

In the jaws of the black cat hung Lilybug, seized at the neck, and the kitten was uttering cries that usually come only from an adult cat. Lilybug had discovered the catnip bushes in the cats' garden and had been rolling in the deliciousness. Tarnish must have sneaked in from the other side of the house, from the field. Now as the kitten twisted to escape, the cat pulled her back toward the field.

Ladybelle had been watching Bouncer's dance from the mulberry tree, which she'd scrambled up in a spurt of playfulness. She came slipping and tumbling down the trunk. But Amarantha was closer to Lilybug. She darted off the steps and sank her teeth into Tarnish's shoulder. It didn't matter that the kitten was not her own. She was the grand old mother cat, and a young one was threatened. The black cat switched around, howling, Lilybug still in his mouth. Ladybelle joined Amarantha, and the two females attacked Tarnish in maternal fury, clawing, biting, screeching. Tarnish let go of the kitten to fight. He caught at Amarantha with grappling claws, and his teeth flashed, snapping first at one female then the other. Black cats and calico rolled and screamed in rage.

As the kitten stumbled clear of the struggle, Sarah, screaming, too, scooped her up. Miss Tabitha ran out of the kitchen with a bucket of water and threw it on the cats. Ladybelle jumped free. As Alexander raced out the back door, Tarnish sprang away toward the field, fur plastered wet and dripping. Alexander tore after him, but the black cat had a good lead.

"Lilybug! Kitty!" Sarah sobbed, cradling the kitten. She wasn't even aware that Miss Jones had her arms around her. The kitten lay limp against her chest. Sarah burst into full wails and tears. Then the little cat stirred. Her head came up. "Mew?"

"Oh, Lilybug!"

Sarah squatted down to examine the kitten. When she touched its paws she found that the tiny pads were damp, as rarely happens, sweating with fear and shock. Spots of blood showed in Lilybug's black fur at the back of her neck where Tarnish had gripped her. But she moved her head easily, looking up for Sarah. There were no other scratches on her.

"Sarah, I think the kitten will be all right," Miss Jones said quietly.

"Oh, thank—thank goodness!" Sarah caught the kitten up under her chin.

An odd crooning sounded. Sarah saw Miss Tabitha kneeling nearby. Before her Amarantha lay on the grass.

"Oh, oh, oh." The old lady's cries were soft.

"Oh, no! Is she dead?"

Sarah saw that she was not. In the moonlight the cat's side sucked in and out in gasps for breath. But Miss Tabitha's moans went on. A tear trickled across the wrinkles in her face, catching the light. As she ran her hand lightly over the cat's fur, Amarantha raised her shoulders, trying to get up. Then the cat fell back, and a red bubble appeared at her mouth. Her sides filled and sank, sucking for air. On the white fur of her stomach was blood where Tarnish's teeth had gouged.

Old Horace came walking stiff-legged and licked Amarantha's face. She meowed weakly to him.

"Oh, my talky old cat!" Miss Tabitha cried. "We must get her into the house."

She and Sarah lifted the cat carefully and carried her into the kitchen. Miss Tabitha found a low cardboard box, and Sarah brought Amarantha's knitted pad to line the box. They laid Amarantha in the box on the kitchen rag rug, and the old lady sank down beside the box, murmuring to her cat.

"Shouldn't we call the vet?" Miss Jones asked.

Miss Tabitha said, "Yes, but—"

"No phone," Sarah said.

"Then I'll go to call."

"Yes, quick! And—Miss Jones, I'm going to stay. Will you tell my parents?"

Miss Jones left, and Sarah ran out to the yard to bring in the kittens before anything happened to them. Ladybelle had them rounded up by the back steps. Horace's birthday party was definitely over. Moonlight lit the deserted yard. The wads of paper were forgotten on the grass as if they'd never been live crackles of fascination, and most of the cats had slipped away to the stable to sleep. Oriole, white in the shadows, still silently hunted under the lilac hedge for only she knew what, and Peter crouched near Ladybelle and the kittens to keep watch. The party mood was gone. As Sarah gathered up the kittens Alexander came out of the shadows, ears laid back, and followed her into the kitchen. In the light Sarah saw that Alexander had no scratches or signs of a fight on his body. He must not have caught Tarnish.

Sarah settled the cat family in its box by the stove. Horace had come in with Miss Tabitha, and he worried around the kitchen, sniffing at Amarantha and retreating, unable to give in to his need to sleep. Alexander saw Amarantha lying in the box, with Miss Tabitha sitting on the floor beside her. Walking over to them, he leaned his nose into the box and made a questioning sound in his throat. "*Mrrt,*" Amarantha answered, but she didn't try to raise her head.

Miss Tabitha hugged the bronze cat against her side. "Ah, Alexander," she cried, "poor old Amarantha is—"

Alexander crouched beside his mistress, and Sarah joined them on the rag rug. As she sat down her stomach growled. She was ashamed to realize she was hungry. Now was no time to be wishing for something to eat when poor Amarantha was so sick. The calico sides rose and fell in shallow breaths. The old mother cat lay with her mouth open, and small puffs of blood showed at her teeth. Miss Tabitha wiped the blood away.

"To end like this!" she murmured. "Such a good cat. 'Rantha, I recall when you were a kitten, snip of sunshine, chasing your tail. And all the kittens you've had, at least two litters a year. Let's see, you must have had more than twenty batches. And four or more each time, oh, think of all your kittens, Amarantha. Such a good mother cat. Such a good old friend."

Amarantha opened her eyes to look for Miss Tabitha and meowed.

Tears were running down Sarah's cheeks, and she said foolishly, "She shouldn't try to talk."

Presently Miss Jones came knocking at the back door. She had unhappy news.

"We can't reach the vet," she said. "Mrs. Bailey says Sam was called over into the next township to look after a sick cow, and she doesn't expect him back until morning."

Miss Tabitha shook her head. "It doesn't matter. I don't think Sam could help. She's bleeding inside, wounded internally. Nothing we can do."

"Oh, no!" Sarah cried.

Miss Jones smoothed Sarah's hair. "I talked to your parents. Your mother thought you should come home, but your father said you must stay with Miss Tabitha if she needs you, all night if necessary."

Sarah looked at the old lady. She had her eyes on Amarantha, but she patted Sarah's hand, saying, "Stay, Sarah."

"Well—I'd better go," the librarian said awkwardly. "I don't see Tansy now. I'll come back for her before the deadline."

Sarah saw her to the door. Miss Tabitha thought to tell Sarah to fix bowls of dry cereal, which they ate beside the box. Horace finally went to sleep in Alexander's rocking chair, and the golden cat kept watch beside his mistress. Now it was only a matter of waiting with Amarantha, giving her the comfort of their presence. Sarah thought once that perhaps they should try to chloroform the cat to end her misery, but Miss Tabitha didn't say anything about it. Probably she couldn't do it, or perhaps she thought Amarantha might recover. It was a vain hope. Through the long hours of the night Amarantha lay dying. Miss Tabitha and Sarah stayed beside her to the end.

When at last the fur sides ceased to rise and fall, Miss Tabitha said, "Good night, my good cat." For a moment she laid her cheek against the many-colored cat, then she placed a cloth over the box. Alexander sniffed once at the box and turned away.

It was too late to walk home. Sarah curled up on Horace's couch in the front room under an afghan that Miss Tabitha brought. The old lady went to her bedroom across the hall. Sarah wondered if she'd cry in bed, but she heard no sounds. Poor old woman. Tears slid on Sarah's cheeks. Amarantha had been with Miss Tabitha so long, and she was almost like a person with her talking meows. She was a good mother cat. It wasn't fair. A good cat killed by a wicked cat. Hatefulness. Hatefulness had won. Oh, what could you do about it, she thought wearily. Tarnish was a wild beast. He only knew what he wanted. Of course she hadn't said "I told you so" to Miss Tabitha. Surely now Miss

Tabitha didn't think Tarnish had some possible good in him.

Horace walked over her, climbing up to his place on the back of the couch. She whispered a good night to the gray cat and reached up for the comfort of his fur, but Horace didn't say anything. He was worn out from the day.

I should go to sleep, Sarah thought. It was hard to sleep in a strange place. I'm going to sleep in the House of Thirty Cats, she told herself. The house of cats was all around her, and she was tucked away to sleep with a knitted afghan like one of the cats. How would it be here when this wasn't a House of Thirty Cats, when there were only three cats? So empty. What would Miss Tabitha do? Would she be so lonely and change and be bitter toward the town? How would she act when Sam Bailey came after all the cats Tuesday? It would be awful to see him rounding them up, hunting them out of the stable. And afterward, hardly any use for the cat garden and the locked thinking room for cats.

It was a good place, this house of cats, this special place. All to be ruined by a selfish old man. It wasn't fair that the badness of Colonel Mace— But it wasn't the same, exactly, as with Tarnish, because Colonel Mace should know better. He was a human.

If only he could turn out to be a crusty old codger with really a heart of gold. Sarah imagined herself talking to him, getting to know him, the way she had with some of the others, finding out his possibilities. If he were really kind underneath, if he could only put up with the cats a little, he and Miss Tabitha could get to be sort of friendly enemies. That way it could even spice up their lives nicely, insulting each other over the lilac hedge in a friendly way. Why, he could be a help to Miss Tabitha, mowing her lawn, mending that broken window.

Sarah warmed to the picture. And then, finally, there could be a cat for Colonel Mace. A—what kind of cat? She remembered her idea of a farmer walking in his woodlot with his vigorous tomcat. Wellington. Wellington, the warrior, should be the cat for a crusty old colonel. They could respect each other. But—she thought doubtfully—a screeching, fighting tomcat was just what Colonel Mace hated. Would he ever unbend enough to get to know Wellington or any cat?

Yet if there were a chance to save the House of Thirty Cats, she should try. She should try to learn Colonel Mace's possibilities. Only—Sarah shrank her shoulders under the afghan—she was afraid of the old man. She didn't want . . . Still, she should try. Look at how well things had turned out when she'd tried to know Mr. Pantiega. And Miss Jones.

I know a little something, she realized. I know a little about understanding people. The way it happened: looking out at people and then looking inside herself to get an idea of how they might feel.

The lookingout-lookingin might work on Colonel Mace. Now if ever . . . She'd try.

Sarah slept.

It was very early when Sarah heard Miss Tabitha stirring in the kitchen. She got up, thinking it was time to feed the cats their stew. Instead she found Miss Tabitha getting ready to bury Amarantha. The body was already in another cardboard box with a lid. The box seemed so small to contain such a fluffy fat cat.

"Now don't cry, Sarah," Miss Tabitha said in a voice that said *she* was determined not to cry. "Bring the shovel from the back porch. I'll carry the box."

The sky was pink with sun about to rise. Alexander followed them out the door, and several cats were already about, lifting their paws from the dewy grass. Miss Tabitha led the way to a corner of the backyard next to the field. Here was the cats' burial ground. Sarah hadn't known it before, for it was only a grassy place. Now she recognized that the stones spaced in a row on the grass were markers.

"Here's a place next to one of her kittens who died young, Hasty."

Sarah dug up the turf. She'd never handled a

shovel, but it didn't seem right for the old lady to do the digging. It wasn't hard anyway. The grass here was long but sparse, old grass.

The sun came up as Miss Tabitha laid the box in the small grave. She talked determinedly.

"Did you know how much the ancient Egyptians thought of their cats? When a favorite cat died, the master of the house shaved his head. The Egyptians mummified their pet cats. Little mummy cats in honorable tombs. They even put little mummy mice and saucers of milk in the tombs for the cats to use in their next life."

Sarah nodded, trying not to cry. She placed the dirt and grass over the box as best she could.

"A marker. I must find a stone." The old lady hurried away. Sarah saw her wipe her eyes.

Sarah returned the shovel to the back porch to leave Miss Tabitha alone if she wanted to be. Alexander, who'd been watching, moved suddenly as if startled. Across the yard Sarah saw a figure beyond the lilac bushes. Colonel Mace was watching too.

So now was her chance.

But she didn't know what to say. She moved slowly across the yard, almost hoping he'd leave before she could get there. Her knees were trembling.

When she was close enough she said, "Amarantha died."

"Who? Oh, a cat." The harsh lines around the old man's mouth deepened in distaste. He went on with what he'd been doing, spraying the ground under his side of the hedge. On the spray can were the words CAT-B-GONE.

Why, he'd ruin the place where the cats liked to play at dusk, Sarah thought indignantly. Then she told herself, No, wait. He doesn't think about how they have fun.

"Shouldn't have buried it," he was saying. "Could have tanned its hide." He sprayed a line along the ground, and Sarah had to move along her side of the hedge to follow him. "Heard of some cat woman once that did that. Every time one of her cats died she had its skin tanned, and finally she had a whole blanket of catskins that she put over her couch."

Sarah listened in horror. How awful. And how unfeeling the colonel was about it. It was hopeless. For Colonel Mace cats were nothing but nasty animals.

But what about people? Surely he was different about people. Miss Tabitha was a human. Surely he had some feeling for people.

"Miss Tabitha is so sad. Amarantha was like an old friend to her."

Colonel Mace straightened up. "Oh, nonsense!" he exclaimed. "She keeps cats. She ought to know cats die. Silly old woman to sniffle."

"But she isn't—" Sarah protested. Her picture of Colonel Mace mowing Miss Tabitha's lawn was fading away. She snatched for it. "Miss Tabitha needs a neighbor for a friend. Oh, Colonel Mace, *please* take back your complaint about the cats!"

"I'd rather move first!" Angrily the old man shook the spray can at Sarah. "And you, you nosy child, stop bothering me! Friend!" he snorted. "That old woman has cats for friends. A neighbor with *good* sense, that's all I ask!" He shot the spray at the ground and turned back on Sarah. "And what do I get? A crazy old cat woman!"

He moved on at his spraying, snorting to himself about "people with *good* sense."

It was a terrible thing that Sarah realized then: Miss Tabitha wasn't even a real person to him. She was just a "crazy old cat woman."

It didn't have to be that way. He'd lived next door to Miss Tabitha long enough. He could have seen all the interesting things about her and how she was a real person. But he was right, and everyone should be like him. That's what he thought. He'd closed off the possibilities. Even his own possibilities, Sarah thought, remembering the nice things she'd imagined about him. He'd always been right, and he wouldn't bend or flower out. He lived strictly by the rules, his own rules. And so should everyone else.

Sarah backed away. She had to get away from

him. He made her feel chilled. Such selfishness. Why, he was worse than Tarnish. She'd forgotten to use the lookingout-lookingin consciously, but she didn't have to add things up. She just knew. Colonel Mace was selfish; he'd bring everything down to his own narrow way.

And now he was closing off all the lovely possibilities of the House of Thirty Cats.

Sarah put her arms around the trunk of an apple tree, hardly aware of what she was doing. It wasn't right. It mustn't happen. Selfishness mustn't win. A person who closed off possibilities shouldn't win. She had to stop him. Somehow she had to save the House of Thirty Cats.

CHAPTER ELEVEN

None of the cats seemed very hungry that morning. Alexander and Horace silently ignored their bowls in the kitchen, and Sarah was sure they were mourning for Amarantha. Still Sarah held the pot for Miss Tabitha to ladle stew into each bowl. Out of habit the old lady started to spoon food into Amarantha's bowl, then murmured, "Oh, no." She stood blankly looking at the bowl while juice dripped from the spoon onto the linoleum. She looked so pitiful that Sarah's heart twisted. That terrible Tarnish. She couldn't help saying it.

She burst out, "Now you hate Tarnish, don't you!"

Miss Tabitha shook herself, and her face came

together in firmness again. "No, I don't hate Tarnish," she said quietly.

"But, Miss Tabitha! Why? He's just fooling you. What possible good is it that you're looking for in that wicked cat?"

Miss Tabitha put away Amarantha's bowl.

"Self-respect," she answered. "He might become a self-respecting cat."

"Self! How can you say such a thing? He *does* love himself. That's *all* he cares about."

"No, my dear. Tarnish is a wild wanderer. I expect people have always thrown boots and hated him. How can he respect himself?"

Miss Tabitha's words drew pictures for Sarah. She saw the gaunt cat wheeling, running from an angry shout, a thrown object. She saw him sneaking in the dark to get his food. She felt how it would be. You wouldn't feel like a good cat, you wouldn't feel the goodness of being Cat. There wasn't any satisfaction, so you kept trying for satisfaction, trying harder and harder to satisfy yourself.

Sarah thought of a stray waterfront cat she'd read about. He'd had a fierce independence, but he hadn't been hateful. Somehow that cat managed to have self-respect. Tarnish had chosen to satisfy self instead, the other side of the coin. He turned it around into getting what he wanted. And here at the House of Thirty Cats he wanted power over the good cats. Maybe he thought the power would make him as good as they. Oh, Sarah knew the black cat didn't think it all out in his brain; he just followed his feelings. Yet he had cleverness. He knew to try to get power over the weaker cats, the young ones, aged Peter.

Miss Tabitha took the stewpot and made ready to go outdoors to feed the other cats.

"As long as Tarnish is alive," she said, "it isn't too late for him to learn self-respect."

Sarah dropped her eyes guiltily, glad that the old lady was going out the door and couldn't see her face. Did Miss Tabitha know she'd planned to kill Tarnish? And yet Sarah felt with a sureness that as long as Tarnish lived—without self-respect—he was an overhanging danger to the peace of the house of cats. Ah, well, there wasn't anything she could do about him right now anyway. Colonel Mace, the deadline tomorrow—those were the nearest dangers. That's what she had to think about now, how to save the cats.

Sarah followed Miss Tabitha out to the stable. Lilybug led the way, perky tail up, eager for this new world of the out-of-doors. But Sarah couldn't take pleasure in her kitten just now. She had to do something, *something,* so this could stay a house of many cats. What *could* she do?

Somehow she had to get those men on the town council to drop their ruling against Miss Tabitha. If only one of the men liked cats. Why did they all have to be on Colonel Mace's side? Nobody likes an animal poisoner. Now what if she went to the men and told them Colonel Mace had put out poisoned meat? But she didn't know for sure that he'd done it. Oh, why couldn't the men on the council feel sympathy for the poor old lady? There were some people in town who felt sorry for her, Sarah knew. How could those men be so hardhearted? How could anyone consider killing fifteen cats all at once! For that was the number left over, fifteen cats to be killed tomorrow.

People would be sorry enough if all their cats disappeared, Sarah thought angrily. What if she could be some kind of Pied Piper, hiding away all the cats in town? She had a quick picture of Sam Bailey with his dog-pound truck, she and Sam driving down alleys, stealing away all the cats. Oh, how silly. He wouldn't do that.

And then there he was. Sam Bailey was in the yard when Sarah and Miss Tabitha came out of the stable. The veterinarian had come to see about Amarantha. He didn't know she was dead.

The old lady told him in a few words. Sam's eyes turned so sad for Miss Tabitha, his freckles stuck out so with his face unhappy (freckles only look right on a happy face, Sarah thought) that he suddenly looked like a little boy.

"Say, I'm sorry, Miss Tabitha," he said. "I should have been here to help."

"No use." The old lady told him about Tarnish and the internal bleeding.

"Well—" Sam said helplessly. He looked into the stable door. "You didn't find homes for all the cats?"

"No."

"Fifteen left," Sarah put in.

"Son of a gun!" he said miserably.

"Do you know of anyone who wants a cat?" Sarah asked.

He shook his head, rubbing his hand over his freckles.

"Anyway, it isn't right!" Sarah was violent. "She shouldn't have to give away all her cats!"

Miss Tabitha patted Sarah's cheek. But there wasn't anything more to say or do. Sarah told Miss Tabitha good-by. Sam Bailey offered to give Sarah a ride to her house.

The morning wasn't so early now. People were out on the streets, going to work, sweeping sidewalks. Sarah looked at them, wondering how many were cat lovers, how many would care whether Miss Tabitha lost her cats. She looked at the young veterinarian, silently driving the car, his face sad.

"Mr. Bailey, how can you do it? You like Miss Tabitha. Probably you like her better than any other grown-up in town does. And you like animals. How can you be the one to kill fifteen good cats?"

He glanced at her unhappily. "Now, Sarah, you

know why. I'm the poundmaster. By law I have to follow the town council's rulings."

She looked down at her lap. "Well, I just don't see how anybody could kill fifteen cats all at once," she said, her voice sinking. It came up again as she exclaimed, "It's all that Tarnish's fault anyway!"

She told him about Tarnish leading the pack of cats, and Sam nodded, for he too had heard reports of a bad black cat. They reached Sarah's house, and it was time for her to get out of the car.

At the last moment she said desperately, "Oh, Mr. Bailey, please try to think of something! Something to change the ruling, to stop the horribleness . . ."

He sighed, but he promised, "All right, Sarah, I'll think about it."

It was a nasty long school day, a queasy-stomach day. Sarah kept trying to imagine up an idea, a plan, something good that would change everything. But her mind either went wild on crazy notions or went fuzzy blank. She simply couldn't think of anything that would make grown men change a law. All she could do was worry. In the midst of lessons, over and over like a litany she thought, "The House of Cats is good; the badness of Tarnish and Colonel Mace mustn't win." Lucy was so sorry for her and hugged her and whispered, "I've got a four-leaf clover I've been saving. I'll wish on it for you." But there wasn't anything else Lucy could do either.

And then when Sarah walked out at the end of school, there was the dog-pound truck at the curb, and there was Sam Bailey standing beside it.

"Sarah?"

Hope! "Mr. Bailey! You've thought of something!"

He laughed. "I've thought of something to make a fool out of myself. Now it may not do any good at all," he warned.

"What? What?"

"Well, it's just that—I'm going to resign."

He explained that when the ruling was first made, he'd supposed that Miss Tabitha would be able to find homes for her cats. But today he'd thought and thought about the old lady and what a fine job she was doing at taking care of cats. He'd thought about what losing her cats would mean to her.

"Well, sir, I just respect Miss Tabitha too much to do this to her."

Sarah gave an excited jump. The veterinarian went on, saying that tonight when the town council met he was going to tell them he'd resign as poundmaster before he'd kill fifteen cats.

"And if I don't do it, who will? You started me thinking, Sarah," he said, "when you wondered how anyone could kill fifteen cats all at once. I talked to old Tom, the garbage collector, and he won't. He knows Miss Tabitha Henshaw's cats and likes them. Let's just see what the council says now."

"Oh, Mr. Bailey!" Sarah seized his hand to thank him and almost danced on the sidewalk. Maybe, maybe—

The town council met every Monday night in a room over the fire station. Sarah said she'd wait in front of the station, and Sam promised to come down to tell her what happened as soon as he'd talked to the men.

Sarah dashed home, and then she didn't know what to do with herself. The time between now and 7:00 P.M., when the council met, was absolutely unimportant. She thought of going to Miss Tabitha to tell her Sam's news but decided to wait until they knew everything. There might not be any point in getting the old lady's hopes up. She tried to concentrate on homework.

During supper an unexpected trouble developed when she asked permission to go out for just a little while. Mother looked very serious, saying Sarah had been out all night *last* night. At last Sarah had to explain everything. It was so hard and mixed-up to tell that tears began to tremble on her eyelids.

And then, surprisingly, it was Mother who reached out a hand to her and said, "This means a lot to you, honey, doesn't it?"

So, while Papa smiled on them, it was Mother who said she could go if she were surely home by nine o'clock.

Sarah breathed a "thank you" and ran out of the

house. The spring evenings were growing longer, and it was still light as she hurried along the streets. She saw the young veterinarian waiting in front of the fire station. He looked nervous, though no more nervous than Sarah felt.

"What if—" she panted as soon as she got into talking distance, "what if one of the councilmen says he'll do it?"

He smiled, shaking his head. "We'll soon find out."

"Oh—tell them how good the cats are," Sarah cried. "Tell them it's Tarnish who's leading the cats in all the trouble!"

"Sarah, I'll do my best," he said, touching a finger to her cheek to chirk it up.

Then he went into the fire station, and the waiting began. And the worrying. *Would* one of the councilmen say, "Yes, I'll do it"? A person might kill one or two cats, but *fifteen?* And be known around town for it? Maybe there'd be some man who could brag "One spring I killed fifteen cats" and laugh about it. Oh, let none of the men be like that, she thought.

Sarah sat on a bench in front, hoping no one would pass and wonder what she was doing there. What I'm doing is praying, she thought. Yet suddenly it seemed so hopeless. Why should the councilmen change their ruling now that they'd made

it? And Colonel Mace, he'd plain have a cat fit (she giggled out of nerves) if they did.

Bong. The clock on the post office tower struck a single note for 7:15. Sam Bailey had been gone fifteen minutes. Sarah watched the hands of the clock move. She wondered what Miss Tabitha was doing with her cats on their last night together. Seven twenty-five. Why was it taking so long? Things couldn't be going right for Sam if it was so long.

Then he came out of the fire station door. His face wasn't dejected, but it wasn't as happy as it should have been if everything was all right.

Quickly, to end Sarah's worrying, he said, "It's good and bad. The council will lift the ruling if—"

"Oh!"

He laughed. "They called me all kinds of soft-hearted fool, but when I asked which one of them would kill fifteen cats, there was a lot of hemming and hawing. Turned out no one wanted to step right up and volunteer to be butcher."

"Oh, I thought so," Sarah breathed. "I hoped so."

They'd talked of hiring someone, but no one could think who'd do it. Sam said he'd had a little unexpected help. It had developed that Mr. Ritchard, husband of the librarian, was an insurance man on the council, and he'd said he rather liked the cat they'd gotten from Miss Tabitha's house.

Good little Felicity, spreading her happiness, Sarah thought gratefully.

"But the bad? You said it was bad too. What about the bad?"

Sam shook his head. "The 'bad' is pretty strong. The council will lift the ruling *if* we can catch Tarnish by tomorrow morning."

He'd told them the black cat was leading the packs, and finally the men had admitted that there had been no real trouble in town with cats until this spring, when Tarnish had appeared. They'd decided ("with some relief at getting out of a hot situation," Sam said with a grin) that if the ringleader were killed, that would solve everything. Then they could report to the townspeople they'd no longer be tormented by cats. As for Colonel Mace's complaint, the men said once Tarnish was killed, Mace would just jolly well have to make the best of living next door to Miss Tabitha Henshaw. After all, she'd lived there for years without trouble over her cats. However, things couldn't drag on forever, waiting for Tarnish to be caught. If Sam Bailey couldn't bring him in by tomorrow, then the council would just have to start hunting for someone who'd kill the cats.

"Rough assignment, to find that cat," he ended, sighing.

"Oh!" Sarah gave a sob of despair. How could they ever find Tarnish by morning! She'd been looking for him all week. Wicked, hateful, hiding cat! Killer!

And then she remembered Miss Tabitha's hopes for Tarnish. His possible good. If she and Sam did catch Tarnish and kill him, he'd never have a chance to learn self-respect. Would Miss Tabitha trade all her cats for Tarnish's chance? If she killed Tarnish, would Miss Tabitha forgive her?

Sarah pulled her mind free of the tanglebush of thoughts.

"We've just got to find him!" she exclaimed.

Sam Bailey kindly offered to spend his evening hunting, and they got into his car. They decided to cruise every street and alley in town. As they drove down alleys in the evening dusk Sarah watched sharply for movements around garbage cans and along the fences. What was that by the telephone pole? Only a gray tomcat. She kept seeing cats, and her heart kept leaping, but never did she see the slinking shape of Tarnish.

Where could he be? Sarah tried to imagine. What would Tarnish be doing at this time of night, this dusk time that was so exciting for cats. Hunting a mouse in the field? Or forcing his will on some young weak creature like Lilybug?

Oh, no.

Quickly Sarah tried to rub out the thought. But the thought was made. Tarnish wanted Lilybug. He wanted power over her. He'd appear if he had a chance at the little cat.

But of course that was too much.

Too much, she insisted to herself. She shouldn't have to risk her own kitten.

She closed her mind to the picture she saw. Watching carefully, she tried to see Tarnish as they drove along. Sam Bailey said things from time to time, and she answered him. But the picture kept trying to come back: Lilybug playing on the grass, Tarnish creeping toward her, Sarah hiding with a sack, ready to jump out and grab him.

It was a way to catch Tarnish. Lilybug could be the bait.

And if she didn't catch him, the house of many cats would be lost.

No, there was still time yet. They might still see Tarnish. He could be anywhere.

"What time is it?" she asked.

"Ten till eight."

She had to be home at nine. She'd wait until eight o'clock. She watched, watched, as they drove slowly. Presently she asked the time again. It was just past eight. She'd wait ten more minutes.

And then it was too late to wait any longer. They were near Miss Tabitha's house, and Sarah asked to be let out. She said she'd look around the house for Tarnish and then run on home. Sam agreed to cruise the streets awhile longer, and he said he'd search again early tomorrow morning. He promised to phone her if he found the cat.

"Any time of day or night," he said, smiling to ease her.

But Sarah felt no ease. She ran down the dark street. No lights showed in the house. This early in the evening the old lady had gone to bed. Was she able to sleep on this last night of having her cats around her? Sarah scratched softly on the back door, but there was no response from within.

The door was unlocked. Sarah stepped over the mop handle on the back porch and into the kitchen. The only light was the reddish-yellow glow of the fire in the wood stove flickering at the vents. The kittens were too big for their box now, and they slept snuggled against Ladybelle on the rag rug. Above them Alexander dozed in the rocker, paws tucked under his tawny chest. As Sarah tiptoed across the floor his eyes opened to yellow slits. He watched her pick the black kitten from the furry huddle of sleeping cats.

Sarah held the kitten facing her. The bright eyes popped open, and the white streak up the nose twitched with alertness.

"Mew?" The kitten looked quickly at Sarah for what fun was going to happen.

"Hush," Sarah whispered. "Lilybug." She ran her finger up the white stripe.

Then quickly she took the kitten outdoors. The moon was coming up, lighting the side yard under the apple trees with whiteness. Sarah put the kitten down on the grass and turned away. Lilybug followed her. Not good. Some apple blossoms lay on the grass, and she blew on them so they moved. Lilybug pounced at the blossoms. She tossed them, caught them back. While the kitten was busy, Sarah stole away to the back porch. The kitten was left alone in the moonlight.

Sarah hid in the darkness of the back porch among the mops and clutter. If she stayed in the yard Tarnish might not come. She'd propped open the screened porch door so she could watch and dash out. From here she could see her kitten hopping about on the grass, delighted with her moonlight adventure, chasing apple blossoms, chasing her own tail. When she darted into shadows Sarah leaned forward anxiously. Lilybug mustn't get out of sight. Good, now she was in the catnip patch, even closer and easier to see.

It was a terrible thing she was doing, putting her own kitten out for bait. What if she couldn't jump out in time? But then Tarnish might not even come. He might be clear across town. Though she was sure he lived somewhere in the field. Yet how could he know that Lilybug was in the open for him to catch? He'll know, she thought. If he's near, he'll know. He keeps watch on this place.

Her hands were sweating. She wiped them on her skirt and leaned back against a stack of boxes, trying to be more comfortable. How long should she wait? She didn't know what time it was.

A passing breeze brought the sweet smell of the lilacs to her and swayed the tree branches. The moving branches made shadows move on the grass and startled her. That—it was only a shadow that moved near Lilybug. The kitten rolled and jumped in the catnip.

That shadow. It was moving. It was still moving, closer, coming on . . . Sarah started forward. Lilybug squeaked at the same moment. The kitten came running toward the house and struggled up the back steps, the black shape darting after it. As the kitten ran by Sarah, and Sarah pounced at the big cat, she realized in a flash that *horrors!* she'd forgotten to find a sack to throw over Tarnish. She'd have to catch him with her bare hands. And in the same split second she tripped over a mop handle. Her hands barely grazed the black fur as Tarnish ran past into the kitchen.

Sarah caught her balance and rounded the corner into the kitchen. The kitten didn't run to her mother. Instead she kept on running, running, through the back hall and up the stairs. Tarnish spurted after her, head down, tail slinking, up the stairs. Sarah so close behind could wonder how the kitten was not already caught, Tarnish was so fast. Yet a kitten could scamper quick as lightning.

Sarah ran up the dark stairwell. The cats could see in the dark. She couldn't. Oh, where—? In the hallway she saw a rim of light under the door to the locked room. Against the light she saw the black shape and lunged forward just too late to catch Tarnish's quicksilver tail as he plunged through the swinging cat panel. She grabbed the doorknob, but the room was still locked. Sarah sobbed in frustration. Her kitten was cornered in the locked room with Tarnish.

As Sarah dropped to her knees she expected to hear the kitten shriek. No sound. The light? Someone in there? Miss Tabitha?

The locked room for cats. At last she'd see it. But in such a horrible way. No time to relish the sight of the room and the mystery it held. Worst of all—what if there was no mystery? Nothing but a bare, empty room. The end of wondering. She'd lost the delicious feeling of maybe-more— No, no time for that. Poor Lilybug!

She pushed open the panel, thrust her head through— Oh, no use! Her shoulders were too wide.

Yellow light. And there before her was Tarnish, slowly backing toward the door, lashing low his tail, snarling. Menacing him, advancing—Alexander! Alexander was in the room, too. Waiting? Had he sensed something about his enemy? The golden cat stalked forward, not a sound from the lips drawn back on his teeth, step, step—Tarnish turned. Sarah shrieked. The yowling black cat was scrambling straight toward her face. She fell back from the opening. Just in time. Tarnish rushed through, and Alexander sprang after him. Down the stairs of the house the two cats plunged.

Lilybug was safe! Or was she? *Where* was she? Sarah put her head through the opening. No sign of the kitten. Hiding? And then Sarah looked at what her eyes had had no time to see before: the room.

Even now it was as if her eyes were taking in a

feeling rather than actually seeing. As if she were looking through her eyelashes, a hazy thing. For there were no sharp details of chairs and tables to see in this room. It was a place of furry softness . . . and warm yellowness. Moonlight poured through the windows that were like yellow eyes, a great cat-eye light. Yet with the furriness there was strength, up and down lines of the walls, like the pillars of Alexander's legs when he sat looking, looking. There was the feeling of purring in the place, rich brown-yellow purring with the throb of a moving heartbeat. A smell, the smell of sun-dusty cat fur. And somehow a flowing movement, the grace of a cat. Slidings, glintings, other feelings she had no words for . . .

Sarah felt out of herself with the wonder of the place. So right it was. This furry, purring room, the heart of the house, this was the very essence of Cat. Here was a place for a cat to go and feel, Yes, this is Catness. I am not all pet or part human. I am Cat. Here is the goodness of Cat.

Ah, Sarah sighed. The utter satisfaction of it.

Shree! a cat shriek from the yard below roused her. Tarnish. She must catch him before he got away! She'd almost forgotten that the safety of the house depended on capturing him.

Sarah rushed down the steps two at a time, clutching at the banister to keep from falling. Miss Tabitha surely must have heard the commotion.

She might be frightened at the sounds in her house in dark of night.

"Miss Tabitha! Miss Tabitha!" Sarah called as she ran through the kitchen. "Come quick!"

A terrible scream rose and wavered in the yard. Then silence.

Sarah ran out the back door. There in the moonlight Alexander rose from the blackness of Tarnish. Stiff-legged he stepped away. The black cat lay tossed on the ground, so still with his legs flung out. On slow feet Sarah drew close to look.

Tarnish was dead.

She couldn't touch him, but she knew it. The sides did not move. She stood still, looking down at the black body. The locked room. It was a place of cat goodness. Was that why Tarnish had been drawn to the room that first time, yet afraid to be there? Too late now. Tarnish's possibilities were ended.

From a small distance the golden cat watched. Sarah looked at him. He had killed. Just for the moment he wasn't the same cat she knew. Probably he had saved Lilybug. But just for the moment she couldn't say his name to him.

"He's dead." The old lady stood on the back steps, a shawl pulled around her nightgown.

"Yes."

Miss Tabitha brought a burlap sack from the

porch and lifted the body into it. The way she picked it up, the body seemed lighter than Sarah expected. She was glad she didn't have to touch Tarnish. But Miss Tabitha said "Poor beast" as she laid the cat gently into the sack.

Then Sarah told her what had happened. In the telling she had to confess that she had seen into the locked room. Happiness came into her voice, remembering.

Miss Tabitha's face revealed nothing. "Did you like what you saw?"

"Yes!"

The old lady nodded. Sarah realized that Miss Tabitha would say no more about the room.

So in a few words Sarah told the good news, explaining what the men on the town council had said about catching Tarnish and lifting the ruling.

The old woman's head lifted. Her eyes were big in the soft light.

"Then it's all right?" she questioned. "It's all right?"

"Yes. Yes, Miss Tabitha!" Sarah cried, the relief of it finally hitting her. "You can still have a house of many cats!"

For the first time she hugged Miss Tabitha.

"Oh, my dear! My little Sarah-Yes!" Tears trickled onto the wrinkled face. "Thank goodness! Thank Alexander!"

He walked to his mistress, looking up at her. She stroked him. Now Sarah, too, could run her hand down his strong back for the cocked tail to meet her hand surely. He was scratched and bleeding in places, but he was all right.

Miss Tabitha went to the cellar to put the sack in the woodroom. Tomorrow Sam Bailey could take it to the councilmen.

Sarah lingered in the kitchen. What would Colonel Mace do now, she wondered. Would he storm and rage, make life miserable for Miss Tabitha? Or would he—she recalled what he'd said—would he move rather than live next door to lots of cats? Anyway the House of Cats would go on being its own special self, a set-apart place in the world. And Miss Tabitha would go on taking care of cats. Sarah looked ahead, thinking of all the strays to be taken in, all the kittens to be raised, all the cats to be given away. She could help Miss Tabitha with the last.

And someday when Miss Tabitha grows very old and dies, Sarah thought, I'll have a little cat carved on her tombstone.

But however had Miss Tabitha made the locked room seem as it did? Already Sarah felt she'd seen the room as if out of the corner of her eye. Had draperies moved in a breeze to give the feeling of a cat's lithe movement? No. She wouldn't try to figure it out. It was like looking at the world upside down between your legs: you could analyze why the world looked so different, but why spoil the pleasure? It's a lovely different view, so you just take it for that.

There was no sound, but Sarah looked up. A small black face popped around the corner of the stairwell in the back hall. Lilybug came stepping off the stairs and ran to Sarah.

"Oh, kitty!" Sarah caught the soft thing against her face. She examined the kitten and found not a scratch.

"So you *were* safe in the room!" Ah, the wonderful room.

Sarah gathered the kitten close to her heart, and then she sat content, with the good House of Cats all around her.

About the Author and Illustrator

MARY CALHOUN was born in Keokuk, Iowa. She was graduated from the University of Iowa, where she also received a Certificate in Journalism. Before settling down to raise her two sons, Mary Calhoun worked on several newspapers. Her hobbies include playing the violin and hiking in the mountains, and she loves to tell stories. She began by writing down some of the stories she told her sons, and her books for young readers followed.

MARY CHALMERS was born in Camden, New Jersey. She attended the School of Industrial Arts (now the Philadelphia Museum School of Art) and the Barnes Foundation. Although she has a long list of children's books to her credit, she considers herself first and foremost a painter, and she has sold numerous paintings and prints.